OUT WITH THE STARS

a novel by

JAMES PURDY

CITY LIGHTS • SAN FRANCISCO

OUT WITH THE STARS

COPYRIGHT © 1992 BY **JAMES PURDY**

ALL RIGHTS RESERVED

COVER DESIGN AND PHOTOGRAPHY BY REX RAY

AUTHOR PHOTOGRAPH COPYRIGHT © BY ELAINE BENTON

LIBRARY OF CONGRESS CATALOGING-IN-PUBLICATION DATA

PURDY, JAMES

  OUT WITH THE STARS / JAMES PURDY

    P. CM.

    ISBN 0-87286-287-9:$19.95. ISBN 0-87286-284-4 (PBK.):$9.95

      1. COMPOSERS—UNITED STATES—FICTION. 2. OPERA—UNITED

STATES—FICTION. I. TITLE.

     PS3531.U426O93   1993

     813'.54—DC20   93-5567

                          CIP

CITY LIGHTS BOOKS ARE AVAILABLE TO BOOKSTORES THROUGH OUR PRIMARY
DISTRIBUTOR: SUBTERRANEAN COMPANY, P.O. BOX 160, 265 S. 5TH STREET,
MONROE, OR 97456. 503-847-5274. TOLL-FREE ORDERS 800-274-7826.
FAX 503-847-6018. OUR BOOKS ARE ALSO AVAILABLE THROUGH LIBRARY
JOBBERS AND REGIONAL DISTRIBUTORS. FOR PERSONAL ORDERS AND CATA-
LOGS, PLEASE WRITE TO CITY LIGHTS BOOKS, 261 COLUMBUS AVENUE, SAN
FRANCISCO, CALIFORNIA 94133.

CITY LIGHTS BOOKS ARE EDITED BY LAWRENCE FERLINGHETTI AND
NANCY J. PETERS AND PUBLISHED AT THE CITY LIGHTS BOOKSTORE,
261 COLUMBUS AVENUE, SAN FRANCISCO, CALIFORNIA 94133.

For
Jane Lawrence Smith
and
Gordon Macdonald

Out with the Stars

Abner Blossom's reliance on his tried and true servant Ezekiel Loomis was never so much valued as when there fell into the hands of the eminent opera composer a dog-eared and yellowed libretto with no name or proof of authorship on it, and no date.

Ezekiel had long since gone off to his home in Harlem when Abner discovered the strange libretto, and he did not like to telephone Ezekiel after he had left Abner's suite of rooms at the Hotel Enrique in the Chelsea section of Manhattan.

But the libretto – it was to change everybody's life! It was as though this anonymous and sometimes illiterate work pointed the way to the very subject for an opera which he had long thought of but never dared to write – or even think of writing.

The libretto kept Abner up all night. In fact he read the stained and foxed, ragged and sometimes jumbled and out-of-sequence manuscript several times. The pages not being in order did not lesson his zeal to follow the story. And perhaps it was after all not a libretto either or a play, certainly not a novel. But the story and the characters Abner knew as well as the back of his own hand. He felt indeed he had written it all down in his sleep or in a delirium.

He could hardly wait until his servant Ezekiel returned the next day.

Ezekiel always served Abner his breakfast in bed. Today Abner had hardly accepted his *café au lait* and brioche from Ezekiel's hand when he popped the question: "Where on earth did *this* come from!" Abner brought forth the miserable looking document like a piece of prime evidence in a court room trial.

"Oh that!" Ezekiel replied in his usual unruffled even slightly condescending manner.

"You say that as if you knew something about it," Abner was more soft-spoken than usual.

. "I did look it over, sir," Ezekiel admitted, pouring his employer a second cup of steamingly hot coffee.

"You read all of it?"

"Guess so." Ezekiel now stood as if waiting to be dismissed.

"Ezekiel, sit down, please."

Abner's respect, almost awe for his servant dated back to the dark November evening of a few years ago when he found Ezekiel reading his French edition of the *Essais* of Montaigne. In fact he had never recovered from his surprise that Ezekiel not only could read French but read tolerably well the sixteenth-century French of Montaigne.

So he was naturally curious as to what Ezekiel had made of the mysterious libretto.

Seated, Ezekiel pretended a diffidence and lack of ease which he did not really feel. If anybody in that household sometimes felt shy in the presence of the other it might have been the dark-skinned Ezekiel's white employer Mr. Abner Blossom.

"I gather, sir, you did read it."

"Several times," Abner now gave out a kind of chuckle. "I thought it had something," he coaxed, "but first of all who in heaven's name left the manuscript here."

"Oh I can set your mind to rest on that, sir," Ezekiel brightened up a bit. "It was your pupil Mr. Valentine Sturgis when he was here for his lesson last week."

"Val Sturgis," Abner smiled faintly. "I see – but what did you make of the play or libretto or whatever it is," he inquired, and as he said this he banged the worn manuscript against his thick comforter.

"It held me, Mr. Blossom. Yes, it held me."

"I can say the same, Ezekiel. I don't know whether the man who wrote it is a writer, or even knows the King's English, but I can tell you one thing for sure, he certainly has a story to tell, and he knows his characters inside and out. They jump off the page for you."

The two men were silent for a while, as if they had found perfect agreement on at least one subject.

"What we must do, Zeke," Abner Blossom said, "is call young Val Sturgis and find out where on earth he found this curious and fascinating opus by an unknown hand."

Ezekiel rose in his rather grand manner, took the tray of empty cups and plates and nodded with a nearly inaudible "Yes, sir."

Val Sturgis was having a late breakfast with his room-mate Hugh Medairy in their Grove Street flat when the call came from Ezekiel Loomis.

Hugh, a singer with a fashionable men's choir, who had come to New York City with Valentine Sturgis a few years back, watched his friend with nervous concern. Val turned a kind of linen napkin pale when he heard that the maestro wished to speak with him.

Hugh stopped chewing on his sweet roll as Val spoke dutifully, almost like a small boy, on the phone. The phone conversation didn't last long and Val resumed his seat beside Hugh.

"Well, what was it about?" the singer wondered.

"Oh, he's not mad at me, if that's what worries you," Val retorted. The two close friends had been having domestic difficulties, and Hugh had once again threatened to leave.

They were both twenty-five years old, and in Val's homely Kentucky phrase, had been through hell and high water together.

"What do you mean it's not about you this time."

"Alright, Mr. Cross-Patch. Let me catch my breath and I'll tell you. Seems that I left a manuscript accidentally at Mr. Blossom's place, and he wants me to tell him where it came from and what I know about the author."

"And?" Hugh asked airily. Unlike Val, he was richly endowed with good looks, a kind of physique seen in the strength and health magazines, and a growing jealousy of Val who was beginning to achieve recognition for his songs and short orchestral works.

"What libretto is Mr. Blossom worried about?"

Val hesitated for a moment, for the libretto in question had rather puzzled him, had in fact haunted him.

"Strange as it may seem, I found the thing on the subway a few days ago. At first I wasn't even going to touch it for it was in bad condition, and quite filthy on its cover in fact. But I opened it up and began to read it and was so absorbed by it I went by our stop here. Ended up nearly to Coney Island in Brooklyn."

Hugh came out of his cross temper and boredom and nodded for Val to go on.

"I was very upset as a matter of fact when I came home the other night to find *I* had lost the libretto too. I had no idea I had left it at Mr. Blossom's. Thought I had left it on the subway like the original owner."

"But what's the libretto deal with?"

"Deal with is right. It's about a famous white novelist who gave up writing novels to become a photographer of all the prohibited subjects in the world, in the 1930s I guess, though the libretto is sketchy on details. But it was, let's see we're now in the year 1965, so it was yes about thirty years ago when the photographer was creating a stir, for in those days even artistic nudes were forbidden to be sent through the open mail."

Hugh Medairy gazed open-mouthed at his friend. Val laughed at Hugh's fascination for the story.

"And Mr. Blossom wants to see you about that?" Hugh resumed his old corrosive tone.

Val nodded. "I hope he's not going to wash his hands of me, Hugh."

"Oh he won't, Val, for cripes sake."

"What makes you so sure?"

"Because he knows if he knows anything, though he's old enough to be your grandaddy, that you've got talent."

"But maybe that's reason enough for him to dump me."

"Who do you suppose this libretto bases the character of the photographer on?"

"No idea in the world."

"I can see you're scared, Val." Hugh finished his breakfast and then stood up. He was late for his rehearsal with the men's chorus.

Val Sturgis also stood up.

"Wish me luck, Hugh," Val went up to his friend.

Hugh hugged Val briefly and then placed a dry very cold kiss on Val's cheek.

"Do you know something, Hugh."

Hugh gave Val an impatient frown.

"You're even better looking today than when we arrived here from Kentucky."

"I bet I'll pay for that compliment later," Hugh smiled in spite of himself and went off toward the front exit, waving a goodbye as he opened the door to go out.

All day long Valentine Sturgis felt a cold dread at the prospect of facing his mentor and teacher Abner Blossom. Abner had been his only salvation in his difficult painful stay in New York City. Val and his room-mate Hugh Medairy had come to the city from a small town in Kentucky. They had studied music at a conservatoire in Cincinnati, and had then with the rashness of those who are quite unaware of evil taken their chance in coming to the metropolis with hardly a spare dollar in their pockets between them.

At first luck had been with them. Hugh more by reason of his good looks than his musical training got a position with a famous men's chorus, and Val Sturgis also through sheer luck became accompanist to a famed retired diva who gave lessons to some of the great sopranos of the day. Val also for a short time had a position with the Metropolitan Opera chorus, but his failure either to show up for rehearsals or when he did show up to come on time soon resulted in his being dismissed.

Valentine felt today as he paced the floor of the Grove Street flat that if Abner also rejected him, he might in despair return to Kentucky where he would, he was sure, waste away.

He could not understand why Abner Blossom should be interested in the strange libretto he had found. Val had lied to Hugh in telling him he had found the manuscript on the subway. Actually he had found it in one of the "parlors" where young men went to abandon themselves to prolonged and delirious orgies. Hugh had warned Val that if he continued to go to these places he would move out on him. Val continued to go to the parlors whenever he could be sure Hugh was away.

In his nervousness over his show-down with Abner Blossom, Val drank cup after cup of strong Italian coffee.

At last the hour arrived when he would have to face Mr. Blossom.

He walked slowly toward the Chelsea area, stopping every so often to chat with some young singer or writer on his way. When they asked him where he was off to, and Val mentioned the name of Abner Blossom the questioner was visibly impressed, perhaps dumbfounded. Abner Blossom was still remembered even then as having composed the most famous opera of its day, based on the lives of Harlem blacks. And everyone knew in the Village that Abner had also singled out Val as the most promising new composer of songs.

Ezekiel met Val at the door, and took his light raincoat with a stony face and inaudible greeting.

"Go right into the parlor, Mr. Sturgis," Ezekiel said after hanging up his coat in a small closet. "Mr. Blossom is expecting you, of course."

"What on earth is wrong?" Abner welcomed his pupil. "You look positively ill. Sit over here where I can hear you better." (Mr. Blossom was suffering from a growing deafness.)

"I hope I haven't displeased or offended you in any way," Val blurted out. "If so I am deeply sorry."

"Offended?" Abner looked puzzled. "Why should I be offended," he wondered, a slight irritation now coming into his voice.

"You have told me, sir, time and again that I often misspeak."

"And so you do. But I am not offended. I am shall we say

intrigued. Indeed fascinated. Look here," he said drawing out from a stack of books on his side table, the opera libretto, "where on earth did you say you found this?" He tapped the wrinkled stained pages of the libretto.

"Oh, that. Yes." Val colored now. "I found it on the subway."

Abner studied his pupil's face, and Val blushed more deeply. "The subway." Abner considered this. "Very well. And did you read it?"

"I read a great deal of it, Abner. Yes."

"How could you not read all of it once you started. I could not." Val began to relax a bit and the color returned to his face.

"And you know nothing more about it than that you found it on the subway."

Val nodded, then he decided to make a clean breast of it now that he saw he was not being accused of anything more serious than having found the libretto.

"I found it, sir, at the Blind Cat night club."

"Somehow I like that better than your finding it on the subway."

Ezekiel entered with a tray and served the two conferees a dark amber something in tiny glasses. Val took a few sips and coughed. Abner sipped his drink and nodded for Ezekiel to leave.

"I want to use it," Abner said in a deep throaty voice.

"I beg your pardon," Val whispered, and Abner, evidently not having heard him, continued.

"I must write an opera along the lines of the libretto you've found. Did you say at the Cat something or other drinking bar?"

"Blind Cat," Val prompted.

"And you don't know who wrote it."

Abner rose and rang for Ezekiel. "Is the tea ready?" he inquired. "Bring two cups then, and the sandwiches."

Eating the cucumber and tuna sandwiches and drinking cup after cup of tea, Abner became expansive. Valentine Sturgis sank back in the cushions of the great chair he was seated in, and listened open-mouthed to Abner's battle plans and stratagems.

"You say also you have no idea about who is the subject of the opera libretto?"

Val assured him the characters in the opera were totally unknown to him. This seemed to please Abner.

"How soon the world forgets nearly everybody," Abner sighed, but it was clear he was glad Valentine did not know or suspect even who the characters in the anonymous opera were.

"The opera, dear Valentine, is based on a gentleman nearing ninety but who is still living and still more active than many men of thirty. The dreadful heroine of the opera is also still with us. *He* is Cyril Vane who was once famous for his slightly decadent sophisticated novels, but who on becoming the inheritor of ten million dollars in 1928 gave up the art of fiction to be a dilettante in photography. But let me amend that. Cyril Vane is actually a brilliant photographer. He has chosen as his field there the same subject he chose for many of his novels, the blacks of Harlem. Amend that to the blacks of nearly everywhere. They stream into his Central Park West apartment. If his novels made him notorious to those sophisticated enough to read them, his photos of the African world have made him one of the most whispered-about persons in all the Great City. His hair shirt and penance for all this glory is his Russian-born wife, Madame Olga Petrovna – who arrived in New York on a cattle boat, they say, with Alla Nazimova – and who, Olga that is, became famous as a silent screen star, briefly about 1915. She still guards Cyril Vane like Argus himself. Is madly jealous of him, but since he holds the purse-strings her power over him is limited."

Abner Blossom now faced his pupil like the defense attorney will at times face his client.

"I want you to go there."

"Where?" Val wondered, spilling some tea on his new cravat.

"To Cyril Vane's of course!"

"For what purpose."

"To be photographed. Despite the fact you are white I will tell him you have the only talent around today for writing songs. He dotes on geniuses even when they're not black."

Like a criminal who has suddenly found his sentence set aside, Valentine broke into short sobs.

"Although I am finishing my cantata *The Kinkajou*,"

Abner went on speaking as if to himself, "my new opera is cut out for me, don't you see? I must write an opera based on Cyril Vane and his jailer, she of the sleepless eyes, Olga Petrovna. It's the idea for an opera I've been waiting for ever since I wrote my first black opera in Paris nearly forty years ago. Valentine, you have been a godsend. May I keep the libretto then?"

Valentine rose now and kissed the hand of his mentor and gulped out, "It's yours, dear maestro. It's all yours."

The next morning Val Sturgis was entertaining his room-mate with a slightly overblown description of his meeting with Abner Blossom on the matter of the lost libretto, but spending most of his time describing the Victorian-Gothic Hotel Enrique with its ornate iron balconies and the regal elegance of its grand interior staircase, not to mention the view one gets from the street of the hotel's Queen Anne roofs and tall chimneys.

"So you're not going then into exile, like all his other pupils have," Hugh broke in, chewing on his croissant stuffed with gooseberry jam.

Val was about to pour Hugh another cup of coffee when the telephone rang.

Hugh answered and then handed the phone to an acutely nervous Val, who immediately put on his "nice boy" act. It was Ezekiel Loomis who was already making an appointment with the song composer.

"But I have my appointment with Madame Elena Baclanova as her accompanist," Val protested.

Hugh heard Abner Blossom's voice then come on the wire. "What do you mean, Valentine," the voice rose. "You have another appointment? No matter who it is, diva or empress, you are due at Cyril Vane's tomorrow at 2.0 p.m. in his Central Park West studio, to be photographed. You can cancel any other appointments, is that clear? And don't come with any of your playmates. Be there alone!" Abner rang off and Ezekiel came back on the wire, and even more pompously read off the address of the photographer's studio.

"Of course you're going!" Val after hanging up shouted at his room-mate when Hugh Medairy protested about his having to be at work at that day and hour.

"If I can cancel my appointment with the Slavic Queen, you can certainly get out of your date with the Men's Chorus. And besides you'll be photographed by the greatest living photographer there is."

Abner's admonition to come to Cyril Vane's *alone* had completely been forgotten by Val at that moment.

"I can see, Val, you are hoping to move in pretty high circles."

Val was astonished at the look of genuine pain and worry on his room-mate's face.

"But if I am going to move in higher circles, Hugh, then so are you. Isn't that right. But don't tell me you're not coming with me tomorrow, Hugh. You can't let me down. After all we've been through together. Listen, listen. . . ."

Hugh edged his way over to where Val was seated and snapped his finger into Val's face. "All right, Val, you win this time. But don't make a habit now of making me lay off work. Somebody has to work around here, doesn't he. And it will never be you."

Having said that, Hugh plopped on his newest Borsolino hat, and blowing a kiss stalked out of the apartment on his way to the Men's Chorus.

The dreaded day, the dreaded hour arrived for Val Sturgis and his friend Hugh Medairy.

The two young men were a bit late when they arrived at the grand if no longer fashionable address on Central Park West where Cyril Vane carried on both his active social life and his profession as photographer. After writing their names in the visitor's book in the lobby they were escorted to the fifth floor by a scowling Irish doorman who looked them over from head to toe and consulted his pocket watch carefully.

The door to the apartment was opened by a dark complexioned man with a downcast but somehow pleasant expression. "Good afternoon," he greeted them, and swung open the door wide. "I am Harlan Yost, Mr. Vane's assistant. He is expecting you in the front parlor, gentlemen."

A very tall man with white hair, and searching brilliantly large brown eyes greeted them with both hands stretched majestically out.

"Which of you young men is the composer?" Cyril Vane wondered.

Hugh almost pushed his friend forward, and Val took Mr. Vane's outstretched hand in his.

"And this is your handsome friend Abner Blossom has also spoken to me about." He shook hands warmly now with Hugh Medairy.

The young men were hardly aware that Harlan Yost had left the room noiselessly and even more noiselessly had reappeared carrying a heavy large tray on which sat two bottles and four heavy Spanish glasses. "I hope you young men will take a libation before we set to work," Cyril Vane's searching eyes never left off staring now at Val and then just as keenly at Hugh.

"May I propose a toast, gentlemen," Cyril began and as he spoke he raised his glass, "a toast to our generous and thoughtful friend Abner Blossom."

Everyone drank, including Harlan Yost, who however seemed to only sip a few drops from his glass.

"I'm wondering however," Mr. Vane looked now nowhere in particular, "if Mr. Sturgis would favor us with playing one of his songs, and if you, Mr. Medairy, would also be so kind as to sing for us." Saying this, Mr. Vane pointed to the back of the large room to a magnificent grand piano.

"It would give me the greatest pleasure, Mr. Vane," Val managed to get out and he took a great gulp of the wine.

"Then let Harlan and me hear you." Mr. Vane turned to his assistant, Harlan Yost who nodded deeply and half-smiled.

The two young men walked resolutely to the piano, and as he sat down on the piano stool, Val looked round at his host and Harlan Yost and was somewhat taken aback at how far off they appeared to be. He raised his hand as he so often did at the Slavic Queen's house and then began playing his latest song.

Mr. Vane was somewhat unprepared for what he was hearing. He had expected something dissonant and metallic in line with many modern vocal offerings, but what came out was rich melody and unabashed feeling. Mr. Vane sank back then in his overstuffed sofa, and closing his eyes smiled faintly.

After the first number, both Mr. Vane and Harlan Yost clapped appreciatively and Harlan cried "Encore." But it was the second and the third numbers which won both the photographer and his assistant over to the performers.

"It reminds me more than a little, gentlemen, of the wonderful popular songs of the 1880s. Wouldn't you say, Harlan I am right." Harlan nodded agreement with an emphatic nod.

After several more songs, Mr. Vane rose, applauding heartily, and going over to the piano he congratulated both performers rather extravagantly.

"You have a fantastic talent, young man. Incredibly moving, immediately communicative!"

The four men moved back to where a table with wine glasses rested. Cyril raised his glass and all four drank in a rather solemn manner which recalled to Val when he had taken communion in his church as a boy. While drinking, however, Mr. Vane smacked his lips in a fashion which somewhat shocked Val. He had never heard a gentleman make such a gross sound in drinking. And then after swallowing more wine, Mr. Vane belched loudly.

"And now to the dark-room, my dear young genius, and your talented friend here, Mr. Medairy. Lead the way," he cried to Harlan Yost and all four exited into the famous studio where almost everybody of note in the arts had posed for Cyril Vane over the last thirty years, including several exiled monarchs, a reigning prince, and almost all the great silent screen stars. There was a definite odor of patchouli present in the room.

A kind of terror came over Val Sturgis as he entered the photographic studio and he all at once reached for Hugh's hand, but Hugh pulled away from him and muttered a word of caution.

Val and Hugh were ushered into seats at the far end of the dark-room. Enormous floodlights now illuminated the two friends. The light was so intense Val could barely make out the figures of Cyril Vane and his attendant Harlan Yost. He thought they resembled figures bidding goodbye to passengers bound for a long voyage on a steamboat.

"And now, gentlemen, our business of the day!" Mr. Vane called to them. "To photograph you for posterity. And, make no mistake about it," he motioned to Val, "you will make a stir in our rather pedestrian frayed era. Remember that, won't you, in time to come."

Drawing closer to Val Sturgis, Mr. Vane exclaimed, "Ah, such circles under your eyes, my dear fellow. Bring the Eau de Bleuet," he addressed Harlan, who vanished almost like a wisp of smoke and returned just as quickly with a large blue imported bottle.

"Move to this seat here now," Cyril addressed Val, "while our good and caring friend Harlan places cornflower water around your overtired and overstimulated eyes."

Harlan Yost administered the cornflower water, and Val blinked wildly and let out a sigh either of relief or unexpected pleasure.

"And now to make a document for the history of modern music," the photographer intoned.

Cyril Vane resembled the conductor of a great orchestra more than a photographer as he stood behind his camera. His hands were strong and white, unadorned with rings, without brown spots, and the nails had a remarkable pinkness. The hands rose and fluttered, then became still. Val Sturgis like all the others who had posed before him felt himself passing into history. A tear came from one of his eyes, although as much from the cornflower water as from the thought he was being immortalized.

"Would you mind taking off your shoes and socks?" Harlan Yost then asked. "Cyril would like one shot of you barefoot."

One of Val's lovers had once remarked that of all Val's best points his feet were probably his choicest endowment and more attractive than his slightly pudgy hands. The wine and the cornflower water gave Val perhaps the courage to remove his shoes and socks.

"Just as I thought," Cyril said. "Your feet are crying out also to be photographed. Cross your legs, please, then."

And so the now-famous photos of the young pianist-composer were snapped of him barefooted, his eyes full of cornflower water, his mouth slightly crimson from wine, his young heart throbbing with pride and joy and an unaccountable fear.

Cyril Vane's eye had however been straying for some time from the less than pulchritudinous Valentine Sturgis to his richly endowed room-mate, Hugh Medairy.

Mr. Blossom had assured Cyril that Valentine would come to the studio unaccompanied. Cyril Vane had tried to act from the first as if he had expected both of the young men, but he began to see from the expression on Mr. Medairy's face that the latter felt neglected. Harlan watched his employer, and saw what was about to happen.

"I am afraid I have been neglectful of you, Mr. Medairy," Cyril Vane spoke at last to the room-mate. "And I would like to correct that now for you are marvelously photogenic. I am sure Mr. Sturgis will not mind if I take a few shots of you alone, will he?" And Cyril gave Val a look of impatient supplication.

"He is all yours." Val surprised even himself by this remark. Hugh on the other hand gave Val an almost withering look.

"Stand over here if you please," Mr. Vane ordered Val's friend.

Val was a little unprepared for the ease and alacrity with which Hugh adopted his different poses.

"Mr. Medairy is perfectly at ease before the camera, isn't he, Harlan?" Mr. Vane now turned to his assistant.

"Mr. Medairy," Cyril began, wiping the perspiration from his subject's chin and throat with a cloth Harlan at that moment bestowed upon him. "I think it is rather too bad to shoot you only with what you have got on. Stylish and stunning as your attire is, I am sure what is under your garments is often more appropriate to the art of photography . . . if, that is," he turned to Valentine, "if Mr. Sturgis will allow us to photograph you thus and so."

Val Sturgis gave a hoarse and nearly inaudible "By all means, Mr. Vane, by all means."

Perhaps it was Hugh's long-pent-up anger with Val, or perhaps after all it was because Hugh had always wanted to be a model and be admired. He stepped out of his clothes with the cool indifference and aplomb of a hardened stripper, careful always to hand each article of his clothing to an efficient and poker-faced Harlan Yost.

"I have never seen such armpits on any model, and, gentlemen, once I even saw the great Sandow in his dressing room. The very word armpit I find wonderfully appealing. It's called *aisselle* in French, *oksel* in Dutch, and *Armhöhle* in German."

Mr. Vane did not need to wait for Hugh Medairy to raise his arms and show the deep but not very hairy caverns of his armpits which had as a matter of fact been praised before by many of his lovers.

It seemed a thousand "takes" then occurred.

Cyril Vane may have photographed Val Sturgis for posterity as a genius, but he was photographing the naked stripped and bare Hugh Medairy for sheer love of beauty.

Val consumed glass after glass of strong wine, and then gradually but completely abandoned himself to the sybaritic extravagance around him. He even laughed occasionally outright and once poked Harlan in the ribs. And in his heart of hearts he was also happy for Hugh. For what Hugh loved above all things else was to be admired, and ogled, praised and extolled for his handsomeness and his manly charm.

And so the evening ended in good fellowship and content all around.

Harlan rejoiced in the pleasure Cyril was receiving from his two visitors. Toast after toast followed, until Hugh began to don his expensive apparel and then bowing low, took Mr. Vane's hand in his and kissed it with genuine gratitude. Val followed his room-mate's suit and kissed both the photographer and Harlan Yost.

And the curtain was rung down on an evening perhaps everybody would recall for a long time. Certainly the two young men who had got out of the visit more than they had ever dreamed of would not soon forget it.

Next day Val Sturgis was on the carpet. Abner had never given anybody such a bawling out. He shouted at Val: "You went against my instructions! Now you've spoiled everything!" Val had reported immediately to his teacher after his session with Cyril Vane, not counting on such a dressing-down from Abner Blossom.

"Excuse me, Abner," Val began, but Abner Blossom raised his right hand in a gesture which would have silenced perhaps even the diva Baclanova.

"Maestro, you give so many instructions, I can't recall all of them at a moment of crisis.

"But what, after all, have I done wrong this time?" Val spoke after a chilling silence from his mentor.

"I told you you were to go to Cyril Vane's house *alone*, didn't I?"

Val, near tears now, gulped, admitting Abner had so ordered.

"Yet you went with your lover Hugh Medairy, didn't you."

"Oh he's not my lover, please, Abner, please. Don't say such things when you're chewing me out."

"But he was your lover, wasn't he. Answer me."

"Oh yes, at one time I guess we were . . . yes! On Grove Street."

"Grove Street!

"Why then did you drag him along. Let me recall my instructions. I told you to go to Cyril's alone and after the usual photographic session I told you to give yourself up to him."

Val repeated Abner's instructions under his breath. At this time Abner was becoming noticeably deaf, but he evidently could read lips and he did not take to Val's repeating his instructions sotto voce.

"You are a fool, Sturgis. A holiday fool."

Val, like many women, found that by weeping he could soften even the angriest of angry parties. He wept on, without however softening Abner's anger.

"Well, you'll be given some beautiful photos at any rate, but your real chance will not come again."

"How could I give myself up, in your phraseology, to a man as old as Cyril Vane," Val wondered irritably as he dried his eyes.

"One must do many things in this life if one wishes to succeed. And I've never met anyone who wanted to succeed as badly as you," Abner went on. "I gave myself up to Cyril after the Great War as we called it way back in 1920. . . ."

A look of such horror crossed Val's face at that moment that even Abner was discomposed. He all at once realized that while Val saw him as old he regarded Cyril Vane as belonging to mausoleums and mummy cases.

"Very well, let's forget the whole business. I have to keep in mind you are talented. You are the only talented young man writing songs that I have met in many years. Of course you wonder why I do not mention your rival Floyd Ormsby. Simply because I don't. Granted his talent, granted his flair, granted his fecundity, but what of Floyd himself!" Here Abner Blossom's eyes flashed with a kind of lightning he very seldom permitted himself.

"I have always admired Floyd," Val admitted.

"I should hope so – but keep away from him. He'll not help you because he will smell out your talent, and he may harm you by being so nice to you you'll not persevere in your own forte, and may try to be another Floyd Ormsby. The world needs no more Ormsbys. Now give me a good-afternoon kiss and get back to your studio and compose. Do you hear, Val. Compose. You've failed with Cyril Vane, but I am still your mentor, and I say Work! Work! For not only is the night coming, dear young man, but oblivion as her handmaiden is not far distant."

At that Val sprang up and grasped Abner's fleshy but powerful right hand on the ring finger of which an amethyst flickered.

Abner noticed Val's interest in the ring and remarked in his dryest tone: "You may kiss my ring, chubby, if you care to." Laughing as a few tears came down his cheek, Val Sturgis gave the amethyst a few quick touches of his lips and departed.

A few days later Abner summoned his pupil Val and without ceremony, without so much as a greeting began: "My producer called on me while you were basking in the limelight at Cyril Vane's," and a kind of alabaster mask fell over the old composer's face. "My cantata *The Kinkajou* is scheduled for public previews next week."

Val rose, eagerly uttering all kinds of words of congratulations.

"Sit down, will you please. One of your worst habits is your effusiveness. You are literally bubbling over all the time. Learn to be quiet, learn not to babble."

Hurt by this stricture, Val looked away and bit his lip to keep it from trembling.

"You are invited of course to the preview."

"But I had no idea your cantata was ready for public presentation."

"Let me tell you something. That opera libretto by an unknown hand has changed everything for me. Don't interrupt now with your enthusiasm. You are responsible for it of course for you left the libretto here. I say again it has changed everything. I've all but lost interest in my little *Kinkajou*, which after all is only a cantata. One reason I believe I sent you to Cyril Vane was to let some of his energy flow through you as his once did through me. You are now absolutely connected with the opera I wish to write.

"It almost makes me believe in destiny. At any rate I can think of nothing but the music drama based on Cyril Vane and Olga Petrovna. I have even begun writing on it. Look here," Abner now got up and walked over to a small cabinet and drew out from it page after page of music score.

"Here is how it begins." He handed Val Sturgis the sheet music.

Val devoured the score, and then began humming and finally singing from it.

"Oh stop for pity's sake," Abner chided good-humoredly.

"This must be your greatest work," Val finally looked up from the score. "It's marvelous, maestro."

"It's all your doing. You must be Hermes in disguise. Before I laid eyes on your stray libretto I felt I was finished. I felt in fact *The Kinkajou* might be my last opus. And now," he took back from Val the opening sections of his new opera, "now it's as if my youth in Paris has returned and with it inspiration I never knew before.

"My producer," Abner continued, after a pause, "wonders at my calm, my impassivity, my far-awayness as he puts it. 'You don't seem to be as fond of *The Kinkajou* as I am,' he pleads with me. Looking him straight in the eye, I reply, 'My dear fellow, I am at work on my major opus, an opera that is, I do believe, grand. *The Kinkajou* is my yesterday, what I am writing today is my today and my tomorrow.'"

Val rose, overcome with even greater admiration for his mentor.

"Here are two tickets for the preview of *The Kinkajou*. I suppose Hugh will be coming with you."

"I wonder," Val confided. "He is very unhappy with me. Says he was treated like Mr. Nobody at Cyril Vane's the other night. Says he always plays second fiddle."

Abner Blossom looked thoughtful.

"Hugh is afraid he is losing you. He's right. Hugh loves you, but you don't really love him back. Not in the way he wants to be loved."

"I suppose you're right, Abner, as you usually are about everything." Val looked sorrowful for a minute, then brightening, "Thanks for these tickets. I can hardly wait, maestro, for *The Kinkajou*."

Ever since the photographic session at Cyril Vane's studio, Hugh Medairy had been glum and taciturn, moody, withdrawn and obviously seething with anger inside. To make matters worse between him and Val Sturgis, every day there arrived by special messenger some luxurious gift from the photographer for Val. One day it was two dozen roses, another some imported bonbons, and yet another time some Swiss linen handkerchiefs. An elegantly wrapped box of Maccaboy Snuff with Hugh Medairy's name on it in blazing letters also arrived.

It was usually Hugh who was handed the gifts by the messenger.

"I can't help it if he sends us gifts, Hugh," Val pleaded as he saw the look of disdain on his room-mate's face. For a moment the anger brought back his original love for Hugh. He would have taken him in his arms at that moment but that he was sure Hugh would have rebuffed him. Hugh's disenchantment was accumulating, had been accumulating long before they went to Cyril Vane's studio.

"We have two tickets for the première of Abner Blossom's

new musical work, the cantata called *The Kinkajou*."

"Yes, I have been reading about it in the different scandal sheets," Hugh said with cutting spite.

"But you'll come with me won't you."

Hugh glowered for a while then muttered: "Oh well, yes. I enjoy scandal also."

"But what do you mean by that, Hugh?"

"Everybody knows what *The Kinkajou* is about." Hugh took a fierce bite out of his slightly burnt toast.

"Why it's about a black preacher in St. Louis," Val almost whispered.

"And a white preacher who is crazy about him."

"Oh, that's hardly given ten minutes in the cantata," Val gave a languid defense of his mentor's work.

"Well, the tabloids seem to think it's *only* about a white preacher smitten with a black evangelist."

"Hugh, I am deeply sorry if you are offended by our session at Cyril Vane's. I apologize if you're feeling hurt. You are now and will always be my dearest friend. Nothing, nobody can change that."

"OK and thanks. Let's leave it at that then."

"Tell me you're not mad at me, Hugh."

"I've been mad at you for a long time," Hugh said, his voice breaking. "Val, look here. We must go our separate ways, maybe not in a day or so but soon. Look, I'm late for rehearsals."

"Hugh, you don't know how what you've just said hurts me."

"You're wondering who will pay the rent I suppose after I clear out. Well, I can always send you a few bucks. Now let's not have a scene. I've got to get out of here or I'll lose my job and then where will either of us find the cash to pay our rent."

Val sprung up and tried to embrace his friend.

Hugh leant down, from his six feet four to Val's five feet eight, and gave him a dry peck on the cheek. "Say a prayer for me too for we're trying out a big new number in the chorus today."

When the door slammed behind him, Val sat for a long

time. He would stare at the roses from the old photographer, and then touch one of the Swiss handkerchiefs still lying in the gift wrapping. Then his eye fell on the tabloid Hugh had been reading, to the place in the paper where the critic had tried to demolish the coming première of *The Kinkajou.*

He read only the first acerbic paragraph.

"My God, what venom," Val said aloud, but then an even greater sorrow was his when he thought of Hugh's terrible goodbye words.

"I know the signs," Val went on speaking aloud, indeed half-singing the words. "Hugh is going to pick up and leave."

It wasn't the worry over who would pay the rent that frightened him so deeply. It was the prospect of being alone, deserted was more the right word, after all their years of struggle and sometimes rapture together.

He could hear again the sound of the door as Hugh had slammed it against him today. A short choking sob came out, then a queer dead silence followed which frightened Val even more.

The small lobby of the old movie house which had been converted to a legitimate theater was crowded with celebrities the night of the première of *The Kinkajou.*

"There's enough smell of perfume and powder in this place to chloroform a horse," Hugh complained as he and Val stood pressed against the front door of the theater. "And smell the moth balls coming from all those mink stoles."

Val hardly heard his room-mate's sour comments as he picked out one after the other the faces of the famous, the once-famous and the few reigning stars of the present.

Then all at once he caught sight of Cyril Vane next to a woman with huge black eyes who seemed to be suffocating in a fur piece which nearly covered all of her person except those strange blazing eyes. Taking the lady by the arm, Mr. Vane grandly approached Hugh and Val.

"I was just telling Olga here that I thought you young men would be among the first to attend. May I introduce my wife, gentlemen."

Olga Petrovna, as she insisted still on being called, bowed very low and threw her head then slightly backwards, then bowing again took first the hand of Hugh Medairy, and then after staring at Val with fierce scrutiny, seized both the young composer's hands in hers.

"You are just as Cyril described you," her voice soared forth in a contralto which drew all eyes to her. "I was bereft, dear boys, at having missed you the other evening at the photography session. It was so naughty of Cyril not to have alerted me you were coming."

"You were in the Caribbean, my darling," Cyril attempted to intervene.

"The next time these charming gentlemen come to our home I must be alerted." Olga actually flirted now with Hugh, dressed to the nines in his evening clothes which he usually wore only for the Men's Chorus.

"And now, dear gentlemen, shall we enter the theater proper for what is bound to be an evening of flash and filigree, tempest, and who knows, cataclysm, but one can never be bored at what maestro Abner Blossom has prepared for us."

At this speech by her husband Olga Petrovna threw at least a half-dozen kisses most of which were directed to Hugh Medairy. Cyril also waved an enigmatic goodbye to the young men, and helped his wife into the first large aperture which led to the reserved section.

"And that is his wife," Hugh kept repeating, staring after Olga Petrovna. "She certainly would not have ignored me so wholeheartedly the other evening of our photo session as he did."

"Oh Cyril adored you, Hugh, more than he did me, but Abner has convinced him I am a genius, that's all his attentions amount to."

Hugh gave Val then one of those strange looks he had been

exchanging with the composer since his warning he was going to move out.

Although their seats were not reserved, by chance they were ushered to a row very close to the Vanes, and quite near enough to hear what the photographer and his wife were saying, for Olga was used to raising her voice to pierce Cyril's deafness.

Val Sturgis found himself in such turmoil over his realization that his room-mate Hugh Medairy was planning to leave him that he barely took in the scope and sophisticated brilliance of Abner Blossom's music. His attention also, like that of Hugh's, wandered to the Vanes. Val's hearing was not as acute as Hugh's, but Hugh kept stifling a laugh at what he heard Olga Petrovna say to her husband.

The audience was divided between adulators of Abner Blossom and detractors and critics who had always despised the now venerable composer.

After one of the most striking songs, delivered by a black bass-baritone, many members of the audience rose to applaud. Among those who did so was Olga Petrovna. To Val and Hugh's stunned surprise they noticed that Cyril Vane himself had fallen asleep, leaning over against Olga's armrest.

Val was also nursing a raging migraine and he wondered if he would be able to sit through the final act. At the intermission, he rose and hurried out alone to the small alleyway next to the theater, where in a few minutes Hugh was able to find him.

"What is wrong?" Hugh scolded, then seeing his friend's condition, he spoke in a quiet concerned tone: "Val, my God you're pale as a ghost." For the first time in his life Val Sturgis keeled over.

He was brought back to consciousness by a policeman and Hugh. In the cab returning to their flat, Hugh held Val's hand in his. "You've been through too much excitement, kiddo," Hugh kept saying.

"I've spoiled your evening."

"Let me tell you something. I was bored stiff by his cantata."

"Oh, Hugh," Val said but felt too weak to argue about the music which he had found transcendent and even thrilling.

When they settled down in their flat the two room-mates looked at one another in an unusually searching manner. They both must have recognized in their exchange of looks that their life together was coming to an end, and a new unknown perhaps bleak future stretched ahead of them.

Cyril Vane was somewhat upset when he realized his two new young friends had left the theater. He kept inquiring of Olga if she had seen them go out. Owing to his deafness Cyril often became perplexed and irritable, and now Olga accused him of blaming her for the young men's having taken leave without saying goodnight.

Cyril and Olga had quarreled during the entire hour and a half of the "musical treat" as Cyril named *The Kinkajou*. Olga's admiration for Abner's work was more moderate though she admitted she could not help admiring it.

"The treatment of the many black personages in the opera is a bit overdone," she told her husband in the limousine taking them home.

Cyril gave her a reproachful look, but then Olga wondered as she so often did nowadays whether he had heard her comment. But when Cyril demurred, Olga raised her voice to say: "The main and perhaps the only reason you admired tonight's musical offering is its subject."

"And what is its subject, light of my life," Cyril wondered.

"Africa of course, Africa," she said resignedly.

"I only heard the music, my dear, as I did not admire the costumes or the scenery. Very much on the homespun side, but then we must remember since Abner is from Kansas City, he may have chosen the maudlin decor on purpose."

"I am glad I went, dear heart," Olga told him. She removed the rose-bud from his buttonhole, and kissed it rather lavishly. "Your two young men recruits are divinely beautiful," she raised her voice. "I do hope I see them again. The taller one is an Adonis," she ventured her opinion.

"But the plainer and shorter one is a supposed genius," he informed her. "Abner's protégé."

Olga sat musing. "Oh to be young again, and to be adored, dear Cyril. How pedestrian are one's later years. How full of effort and strain, and sameness, sameness! It's the sameness I cannot abide."

"Now, now, sweet, don't let it overwhelm you like this. Am I not here?" He hobbled over to her chair and took her hand in his. "Ever faithful, my darling, ever faithful."

"Why are beautiful young men so depressing, Cyril?" she wondered.

"Depressing, dear? Don't you mean perhaps tantalizing?"

"Oh have it your way," Olga pretended to pout.

They kissed in a kind of rapid pecking manner which recalled birds billing and cooing from separate cages.

And at that moment an attendant entered with their brandy and their watercress sandwiches.

All day long a crowd had been collecting in front of the hundred-years-old Hotel Enrique. Some of the persons assembled were curiosity seekers, others were angry because they felt *The Kinkajou* had disparaged African Americans, others were simply angry at life in general. But all of the crowd was spoiling for trouble.

The police were called several times, but finally deciding the crowd were autograph-hunters or harmless idlers, departed in a blare of sirens. But toward evening, with a cold needle-like rain falling, the crowd pushed into the hotel lobby itself and rushing by the two small elevators began ascending the broad palatial iron staircase to the ninth floor where the composer had lived for over forty years.

A frantic hotel clerk had rung up, warning Abner that troublemakers were marching upstairs to his suite, and some of them might be dangerous and perhaps even armed.

One of the qualities Abner's friends admired in him was his pleasure in an altercation and his readiness for a fray. So that far from being afraid that a mob was about to push its way into his suite of rooms, Abner boldly opened the door when he heard the footsteps approaching, and stood arms folded at the head of the stairs.

His scowling mien and calm even regal manner caused the trespassers to halt and for a while they became sullenly quiet.

"Speak your piece, gentlemen, and I see a lady or two also. Tell me to what I owe this delegation."

The crowd was mesmerized by this small man who resembled, all five foot two inches of him, Humpty Dumpty who had willingly come down from the wall.

But Abner Blossom had something else which halted and becalmed them. It was the assurance he was always right, the absolute confidence he had no equal, and the calm which comes from implicit belief in his calling and mission.

He stood therefore on the interior grand iron staircase, praising shamelessly his own work, extolling *The Kinkajou* as superior even to his first Negro opera of some thirty years before, and he read encomiums from titled persons and crowned heads concerning his genius and then, to the astonishment of the assembled crowd, sang out one of the arias from *The Kinkajou*. As his voice died away, the once-angry mob, relaxed and moved and changed by his personality, his supreme generalship (Alexander the Great was also of short stature), involuntarily burst into applause.

Ezekiel Loomis and another servant now emerged from Abner's suite, bringing cups of imported cider, and cookies, which they handed round to the spell-bound invaders.

Without one dissenter, the recently infuriated mob now drank to the health of the composer, and before turning tail praised – perhaps excessively – the work they had come to condemn.

The next morning the press recounted in detail the attack on the ninth-floor suite of the composer, and the success of *The Kinkajou* was assured as much through scandal as from merit.

Every time Hugh Medairy left now for the Men's Chorus, Val Sturgis feared he would never see him again. The imminent loss of Hugh restored almost to its full strength Val's love for his room-mate. And with the revival of his love came a cold dread, even terror of what was to become of him financially. He had not earned enough from his accompaniment sessions with Madame Baclanova even to pay his rent. For a while, he recalled, he had been a member of the Metropolitan Opera chorus, where his incessant tardiness and his inclination to gossip about stars no longer in their prime earned him a final dismissal.

Val Sturgis was always losing his jobs, always living hand to mouth. His being praised by Cyril Vane and Abner Blossom had for a while turned his head. But genius does not insure a meal ticket. The day after the première of *The Kinkajou* Val sat for a long while in a kind of funk that was almost paralysis.

After a few hours he went down to the corner news-stand and picked up as many newspapers as he could afford. Coming back to his apartment he began reading with trepidation about Abner Blossom's première. But before he could read any of the reviews he saw the photographs of the crowd's attack on Abner's suite in the Hotel Enrique.

There in a huge partially tinted photo was Abner facing a crowd of young singers, actors, schoolboys, society dames and hoodlums with the composer looking as fierce and in charge of everything as a general leading his troops.

Val burst into appreciative laughter. He forgot for a while his own desperate situation. Then turning the paper he saw a long laudatory article on *The Kinkajou* by Cyril Vane himself. And Val was as pleased by what Mr. Vane had written in praise of Abner's music as if he were reading an encomium about his own songs.

Val Sturgis came to realize in some strange way which he himself was unable to understand that he loved both these old men, and he felt that their sudden appearance in his life was a godsend now that he was losing Hugh Medairy.

A week or so passed in which Val watched with a kind of feverish concentration the signs of Hugh's coming departure. Valises brought out from God knows where, hat boxes, arranged in order, and chiffoniers emptied of their expensive shirts and imported handkerchiefs were everywhere in evidence.

Val could not compose while waiting for the final blow. He drank pot after pot of the Arabian coffee Mr. Vane had sent him. He read and reread all the reviews of *The Kinkajou*. Even the most scathing ones implied Abner Blossom was a composer of undoubted talent and scope.

"Mr. Blossom probably has forgotten I exist," Val whispered to himself.

Every so often the thought of suicide crossed his mind. The burgeoning fame of Abner Blossom made his own songs seem like thistledown in comparison.

Then in the midst of his deep sorrow and discouragement the phone rang insistently. He decided not to answer, but then as the ringing did not stop he took up the receiver. Ezekiel's voice boomed out into the room littered with hat boxes and luggage.

"Mr. Blossom wonders why you haven't called," Ezekiel chided. "He would like to see you this afternoon. He won't take no for an answer."

Val Sturgis almost sobbed his words of acceptance.

Ezekiel Loomis ushered Val into the composer's study a few hours later.

"Thank you for the posies you and Hugh sent me," Abner began at once. "You are dears, both of you."

Val mumbled some words of rejoinder and then becoming apprehensive waited for what might be another blow to fall. (He had never forgotten the stories that Mr. Blossom eventually washed his hands of young talent.)

Ezekiel brought in some sandwiches and two bottles of French beer.

"I adored your cantata, maestro," Val began, emerging a bit out of his depression. "The arias never leave me."

"I know you mean that," Abner replied, softening.

"I haven't offended you in any way, have I?" Val plunged in all at once. "I know I sometimes . . . misspeak."

"Offended me? What on earth are you talking about." Abner looked dumbfounded. "Of course you haven't. Drink up your beer or it will get warm. Ezekiel, bring us another two bottles if they're sufficiently cold.

"The damned Europeans drink their beer almost tepid," Abner said nervously. It was clear he was coming to something, and Val wondered what new blow might be in store.

"You mustn't admire me, though, Val Sturgis, too much," the old man now began once Ezekiel had brought in the two fresh bottles. "It won't do. It must not occur."

"But I don't . . ."

"Listen. You must not be another Abner Blossom. The world does not need another Abner Blossom. The world does however need a new Val Sturgis."

Val grinned broadly and sipped the cold French beer.

"I know your admiration for my music is sincere. Maybe even deep. Cyril Vane has told me he is sure you worship me. Well, that won't do either, will it."

Val's worries now increased, and he looked rather helplessly about the studio.

"You need a teacher, Val. I'm too old and busy to take up the task. Had we met thirty years ago I would have been the one to look over your shoulder as you compose. But there is another reason I am not as much at leisure as I might be. And you are responsible for my being no longer free."

"I, maestro?"

"You, you. Who but you."

Sipping beer and biting into his sandwich, Abner went on trying not to look at Val Sturgis's troubled countenance.

"The lost libretto. Or the lost libretto that was found and given to me. It has changed everything, Val. I can think of nothing but it."

"You mean . . ." Val gulped and choked.

"I mean yes I am writing an opera based not so much on that dog-eared illegible libretto but on the characters the librettist clearly had in mind to write about. Cyril Vane and Olga Petrovna! They're my opera. And you have brought it all about."

In his astonishment Val Sturgis suddenly stood up as one does when a renowned singer has given forth a great aria. Seeing how queer his rising must seem, he sat down with a kind of collapse.

"I've begun already, and so I won't be quite as free and at leisure with you as we've been. But we will always see one another, Val. By the way what's troubling you."

"Oh nothing much except Hugh Medairy is leaving me after all the years we've been together."

"Ah, ah," Abner thought this over. "Trouble they say always comes in pairs or is it threes. None the less, Val Sturgis, you have me for a friend. Rely on me. I won't be that busy for anyone with your talent."

Val looked down at his shoes which he had forgotten to shine for the occasion.

"I have found you a teacher." Abner Blossom brought out now what was the occasion of his summoning the song writer.

"Yes, maestro," Val said hardly comprehending what Abner was talking about.

"You're too dependent on me, Val," the old man softened now. "Don't think I don't love having you care that much. But it's not good for either of us.

"You need a teacher, Val."

When Val began to protest, Abner became severe.

"As I said, a teacher but not any teacher mind you. I wouldn't send you to just any teacher. You know me better than that. But Val, though you have talent, for it's coming out your ears, you lack discipline. . . . Don't blubber, I won't have a blubberer on my hands. That's what is wrong with your music when it is wrong, which isn't too often, but even once is too much. You have too much emotion! You are frequently on the verge of tears like some ladies. Stifle those tendencies. Be perfectly above it all. That is why I am sending you a Polish gentleman who lived in Paris for many years. Broke his hip though somehow or other, and now uses a crutch. Composes himself. Symphonies and other things. I'm not too sold on them, but still. . . . He is a true teacher however. As I say, I knew him in Paris. He's not old either, and is very handsome. But beware of his wife, Laetitia. She's as jealous of him as a lioness of her cub. Thinks every person who enters their tacky studio has come to go to bed with her prince and idol, Harold. Beware therefore of Laetitia. Take her sweets when you do go, compliment her on her fading alabaster beauty and her still stylish blond hairdo – she's Polish too. But she'll watch you like a sparrow-hawk. So don't flirt with Harold. And work! He'll teach you, but you've got to work. Don't let people think you have a chocolate eclair for a spine. Work off the sugar in your life and your music. Be spare, be sharp, hit the bull's eye, don't flounder, and quit using so many notes in your songs. Too many notes will drive your audience into the streets. Now here is his telephone number, and I've already told Harold you are coming. Are you bawling again, for mercy's sake?"

Abner stepped over to where Val sat sniffling with gratitude, with fear, reverence, and of course love. His tears blinded him to the telephone number, but he took it, and kissed Abner full on the mouth and Abner smiled at the embrace.

"Now behave yourself and work. It's not love which makes the world go round. It's slave labor."

Harold Reszke had almost blindingly blue eyes, a strong nose with flaring nostrils, and a kind of cornsheaf of billowing yellow hair. His arms, always on the massive side, had become Herculean by reason of his using a crutch to hold up his considerable frame and weight. He smarted continually from his injury, for he had been somewhat of an athlete. He motioned Val to the piano stool as his only greeting.

Sitting stiffly before the keyboard, Val could hear dishes being moved about in the kitchen, and water running, then sighs and sniffles, followed by a kind of grumbling.

Harold rose with injured dignity from the chair beside the piano stool and banged close the door from which the dish-washing sound had arisen.

"Now play me your latest song, will you please," Harold commanded.

Val plunged in. Harold closed his eyes, and his head moved dramatically in time with the music. Then all at once, he cried, "Stop there, Mr. Sturgis. What are you changing keys for and what is the meaning of this section?" He pointed bellicosely with his crutch to the keyboard.

"Ah," Val sighed, remembering what Abner had found at fault with his music.

"Aren't you saying too much, and have you not made a detour from your opening section, Mr. Sturgis?"

"Please call me Val."

"We will see," Harold said, and he began writing some notes down on a piece of music paper.

At that moment Laetitia entered, and stared lengthily at the newcomer. Val turned a languid look toward her, and nodded.

She wiped her sudsy hands on her apron, scowled, and hurried from the room.

"Now, Mr. Sturgis," Harold was so majestic and hand-some at that moment, Val lost all train of thought, but a blow from the crutch on the floor by his leg brought him back to harmony and counterpoint.

"Sit over here," Harold Reszke ordered Val.

Val sat in a chair as far away from Harold as he could for he remembered Abner's warning and the scowling look Laetitia Reszke had given him dampened his spirit.

"Well, what are you doing ten feet away, sir," the teacher raised his voice. "I want to go over your new song which Mr. Blossom sent me the other day. I've jotted down a few things here for us to go over together."

In his confused state Val could barely decipher what Harold had written down for him to read.

"This is a very beautiful passage here," Harold Reszke pointed to the second page of the score. "You've set this for soprano of course."

Val nodded. He could feel the teacher's breath touching his hair.

"I didn't mean to shout at you just a few minutes ago," Harold Reszke apologized. "Let me tell you, sir, you do have talent, just as Mr. Blossom has testified. Maybe more even. . . . But look here now."

The teacher inquired why Val had put such a long part for the piano at the end of the song.

"Would you consider abbreviating that section perhaps, or do you even want such a long piano finale there. Do you see what I mean?"

Val was aware then that the teacher had placed his large powerful left hand uncomfortably on Val's shoulder. Harold Reszke went on pointing out here and there notes which he thought could be changed, or best omitted.

"You could very easily transpose this beautiful song for the male voice one day." Harold spoke throatily and his left hand with the wedding ring handed back the sheet music to the composer. Then moving violently in his chair Harold got out, "Will you work then, sir, on the changes I have suggested?"

Val nodded painfully, overcome with gratification. He had found someone who both encouraged him and yet held him to the only discipline he had ever known.

"Are you sure you heard what I just said to you?" Harold demanded in his booming voice.

Val nodded and choked out a "yes."

As Val gathered up his sheet music he came then face to face with his teacher. All at once standing without his crutch the teacher by reason of his great height and the strength of his arms gave the impression he was towering above the younger man as if on some raised platform, such as one saw in music dramas.

Harold grasped Val by the shoulders, almost shaking him.

"Come tomorrow," the teacher said in a voice loud enough

to be heard in the next room.

"Let me tell you again, Val," the teacher went on. "You have a real talent – a true gift. Nourish it, live by it – do you hear me?"

Motionless, unable to respond just then, Val could only look into the eyes of Reszke.

"Come tomorrow, and bring the corrections," Harold resumed his stern almost angry tone.

Babbling thanks, confounded by such praise and kindness, Val rushed out of the room.

In the hallway leading down to the front stairs, Val dropped all of his music. Hurriedly stooping down, hands trembling, he began trying to gather up the sheets of music in order to put them into his attaché case.

All at once he could hear Laetitia's voice raised in a kind of fury. "Do we have to have someone like that traipsing in here?" Harold Reszke's wife shouted. "Are we that hard up now? I might have known, any pupil of that old pederast Abner Blossom would be paying court to you! The minute my back is turned, and you are all by yourself!"

All at once Harold could be heard shouting wildly, and his shouts were followed by squeals and whines from Laetitia as Harold slapped her. Val crept on down the stairs. At the front door he paused. He was out of breath and so confused he hardly knew in what direction to turn to take the way back to Grove Street.

Going home Val began to come out of his conflicting feelings about his afternoon with Harold Reszke. All at once it became clear: he had found in this teacher someone who would both encourage him to compose and who would also correct his faults and discipline his talent. He felt a deep gratefulness to Abner Blossom for having introduced him to Harold, and the unpleasantness of Laetitia's outburst was forgotten. He could hardly wait now to share his good news with Hugh Medairy. Though Hugh was he feared a bit jealous of Val's burgeoning talent, he could always count on his room-mate to share his happiness and good luck.

In his excitement at the door of the flat, he dropped his

keys several times before he could put them in the lock. Opening the door at last he rushed in. He was about to call Hugh's name, but there was a kind of indefinable but palpable change in the room's atmosphere. There was even a different smell as if he had opened the door to someone else's apartment.

He put down his attaché case and his keys and stood looking about him.

"Ah, yes," he spoke like someone explaining the change to another person.

All the valises, hatboxes, packages were gone. The apartment itself looked nearly vacant except for the upright piano.

Going toward the tiny kitchen, Val sat down heavily and loosened his tie. His feet hurt from the long walk and he removed his shoes.

Hugh had finally gone! A hurt like that from some sharp instrument against his chest drew a kind of faint sound from his tense mouth and jaw, a sound he had never heard himself make before. Yes, he had known of course that Hugh would leave, but he had never believed it until now. His oldest, most dependable friend had deserted him.

He felt at that moment he had no one in the world.

Then on the big deal table he caught sight of an envelope with his name in Hugh's handwriting. The envelope had not been sealed, and a note on expensive stationery fell out. Val read:

I will never forget our years together, will never forget you, Val. I will always care. But my own unhappiness with you was beginning to make me lose my deep love and appreciation for you. Do you understand, dear friend. Call me at the following number and address.

The notepaper fell from Val's hands. Looking about he saw that it was past evening now, the deep night of the city was everywhere.

He did not bother to light the center light.

Lethargically he picked up the notepaper and stared at the message. His boyhood, perhaps his youth even was over. They had come to the Great City, Hugh and he, to make their fortune. A choking sorrow and depression came over him.

Then he thought of Harold Reszke, as the only light at the moment in such sorrow.

Leaving the apartment he began walking toward West Street in the direction of the water. Some of the street lights had gone out making the night truly oppressive and black. Before he knew it he was standing on the docks, which people in that neighborhood called Suicide Docks.

The thought of suicide was not new to Val. His and Hugh's life had been nearly unendurable at times, never easy. Then he thought of Harold Reszke's encouragement, and he thought also of Abner Blossom's kindness. He looked at the still, black water, then turning abruptly he made his way back to his empty flat.

From that day on, Val Sturgis did nothing but compose. Sometimes he stayed up all night falling exhausted when the early morning light streamed into his Grove Street flat.

He put away the photo of Hugh Medairy, taken by Cyril Vane.

Every day except Sunday now he came to Harold's place and showed him his new songs. Harold would sit down at the grand piano and play them. Sometimes he would stare at Val in a kind of stunned wonderment.

"You wrote all these since you have been coming here?" Harold would always repeat this statement. Then he would smile slowly and shake his head.

Val wondered where Laetitia was now during their lessons, but had not the courage to inquire. His relationship with Harold was becoming strained which reminded him of his last days with Hugh. He wondered what he would do if Harold suddenly also closed the door on him and there were no more lessons and who knows perhaps he would write no more songs.

One day almost out of the blue while Harold was going over one of the songs he had written the day before, Val blurted out: "Do you know, sir, that Mr. Blossom is writing a full-length opera."

Harold put down the sheet music and looked at his pupil with a half-humorous, half-baffled expression.

"What is the subject – do you know?"

"The subject," Val spoke with embarrassment and a flush spread over his face. "I'll try to explain. . . . A while back I found a libretto. It had no clue on it as to its author or when it was written. It was in very bad condition. I read it with fascination. Then, absentmindedly, one day I left it behind at Mr. Blossom's." Val stopped, fearing he was giving away a secret.

"Go on," Harold said, and rising, not bothering to use his crutch, he came over and sat beside the song composer.

"Mr. Blossom was even more taken with the libretto than I had been. He began then immediately writing his own libretto based on the one I had found."

"But what is the subject – I asked you," Harold evidenced impatience and growing irritation.

"I don't know I should tell you."

Harold made a sound of extreme displeasure and Val recalled the furious anger he had shown toward his wife on Val's first visit to the Reszkes'.

"It concerns the photographer Cyril Vane."

"Cyril Vane!" Harold gasped and his face took on an entirely different color and expression, the veins in his eyelids appeared flushed and his lips closed tightly about his teeth.

"How on earth did you ever hear of him?" Harold spoke softly now perhaps trying to control his emotion.

"I was photographed by him," Val said.

Harold had gone rather pale in contrast with the flushed color of his face a few moments before. "Go on," he said in an almost inaudible tone.

"That's all there is to it. Mr. Blossom thought my roommate and I should have some good photos, so we went to Mr. Vane's studio."

"And your room-mate has left you I believe you told me last time."

Val nodded.

"I am surprised that Mr. Blossom would send a young man like you to meet Cyril Vane," Harold had regained his composure, but he had taken on a distant, formal, almost hostile calm.

"Anyhow you have your songs," Harold said at last. "Nothing, nobody should be able to take away your talent."

"Excuse me, Harold," Val began, still uneasy he had permission to call his teacher by his first name.

"Yes," Harold encouraged him when the song composer failed to go on with what he was saying.

"Did you also know Mr. Vane perhaps."

Harold colored again.

"I met him in Paris years ago. Before I was married."

"And did he photograph you also?" Val spoke in a kind of whisper.

Harold nodded, and then rising, reaching awkwardly for his crutch, he sat down at the piano. He began playing Val's latest song. After he had finished, Harold turned to his pupil: "These last songs have something deeper in them, Val. You are growing right before my eyes! It's incredible! Do you realize what you are doing. Of course not! Listen, go home and write me something new, do you hear. Write another song."

Harold Reszke looked at the wall clock, indicating the lesson was over.

In saying goodbye today, Harold took Val's hand in his and pressed it painfully, holding it a long time.

"What does anything matter to a man who has your talent," the teacher said bidding him a final goodbye.

In the days that followed Val Sturgis did nothing but compose. Sitting at the piano he first of all played anything which came into his mind, and then when he had hit on something which he felt expressed everything he was feeling, everything perhaps which he had ever felt, he took out his music paper and frantically tried to put down all the notes which had been pouring out of him as he sat at his broken-down piano.

He wrote for hours, and then looking back on what he had written he went to a messenger service and had the new song sent at once to Harold Reszke.

The next day a similar thing happened. Whether it was Hugh Medairy's having deserted him or Harold Reszke's amazing encouragement and kindness, he was in a kind of delirium of work, possessed of an energy which appeared to have no cessation.

During the early morning hours he played what he was feeling, letting his fingers find by themselves what his own words and heart did not dare tell. Then he would rush to his music paper and attempt to write down all he had heard come from the keys of his wretched piano.

Again he would take the manuscript and send it to Harold by messenger.

Worn out then he would lie down on an old mattress placed upon the floor and look up at the high ceiling. Then in utter exhaustion he would fall fast asleep and sleep on for twelve or fourteen hours.

One evening as Val was brooding and drinking cup after cup of the Arabian coffee sent him by Cyril Vane, he heard a very faint tapping at his door. Thinking it probably was the man who cleaned the halls occasionally he paid no attention. The tapping became louder then and more insistent.

Dragging himself to the door he asked in an irritable tone who it was.

Harold's voice replied.

Val flung open the door.

Harold came in without a word, and sat down at the piano.

He played a few chords and smiled.

"Did you read what I composed?" Val watched his visitor with growing uneasiness.

"So this is where you live, and have your being." Harold then brought out from his satchel the songs which Val had sent him by messenger.

Val stared at the manuscripts.

"Don't pretend you don't know what they are worth, Val," Harold spoke. "I played them myself on the piano. Played them is not the word I guess. Anyhow I have lived with them from the day they arrived. They are not only beautiful, Val, they are faultless."

"Faultless," Val repeated. He sat down beside his teacher.

"Do you have anything to drink," Harold wondered. He wiped his forehead with a cloth he took from his hip pocket. "Managing this damned crutch up all those stairs," he muttered.

"I have some brandy, Harold."

"Brandy will be just the ticket."

Val brought out one of the bottles of French cognac which Cyril Vane had bestowed on him and two glasses.

"Ice?" Val tried to keep his voice from quavering.

"Don't bother." Harold opened the brandy bottle and poured the two glasses. "Val, listen to me. Listen carefully. Tell me, have I given you something?"

"Given me something." The composer looked away. "What a question." He drank hurriedly from his glass. "You've given me everything. Do you know how much you have? You've been my salvation after Hugh left. You've. . . ."

"I hoped you wrote these latest songs because of our – friendship."

"Friendship, Harold! I think you must be my Muse."

This remark appeared to trouble Harold Reszke. He poured himself another cognac.

"Val, pay close mind now to what I am going to say. I am not your Muse. Maybe I awakened her perhaps. But you have your Muse. You don't need me, Val. You don't need anybody. Don't you understand? I believe maybe you don't. No matter. Val, you have your whole life and career stretching before you. You don't need me. Look what I am." He stared wildly at his crutch. "I might have been your Muse once in Paris, but there is such a thing as destiny."

"Thank God you liked the songs, Harold," Val felt a growing apprehension, and he made this remark only to prepare himself for what he felt was some fearful pronouncement from his teacher.

"*Like* is a pallid word for what I felt. You have brought back to me my own youth and hopes. When I played your songs I thought I had written them . . . in Paris. The truth is I will never write anything again."

Harold stood up shakily.

"Do you have any coffee," the teacher wondered, and took up his crutch. "Make some, will you, while I use your WC."

Val stood for a while in a vortex of conflicting feelings. He knew something more was going to be said, something as shattering as Hugh Medairy's farewell note. Turning to his small stove he put the water on to boil, and measured out the tablespoons of Arabian coffee. The brew was ready when Harold returned.

"No cream," the teacher spoke in his old severe tone.

They drank the black coffee for a lengthy while in silence, and Val rose at last and made another pot.

"What do you want to tell me, Harold," Val said brokenly.

"I know you know, Val," Harold said. "Wait until you are married," he added.

"I will never be married, Harold. You must know that."

"No one knows that," Harold said. "How can I tell you."

"Please just say it. You're hurting me too deeply in postponing your message."

"Message?" Harold scoffed. "See here, Val! I cannot go on being your teacher. Don't ask me why. Don't. . . ." Harold began to rise.

"Sit down," Val spoke in a manner and voice Harold had never observed before. "You don't need to tell me why but don't go. Wait until I have quieted down."

"Do you think if I didn't need this," Harold struck at his crutch, "do you think if I was what I was in Paris, I would be telling you I can't teach you any more. But you're not looking at the young composer Harold Reszke, the one both Cyril Vane and Abner Blossom were so taken with and whom Cyril Vane photographed. No, you're looking at somebody else, somebody I don't even know or care about."

"But you can't just end our friendship like this. I mean –"

"Friendship is a pretty poor word for it, Val."

"And I don't know what I'll do if you won't see me and hear my music."

"I've told you what it is, Val, but you don't understand. It's her, it's Laetitia. She's all I have and she won't let me share her love with anyone else."

"But it's more than love, isn't it."

"That makes it all the worse then."

But gradually even as they spoke Val Sturgis was retreating from his teacher. It seemed later to Val that he had moved into another room as the teacher was choking out his explanation, his apology, his farewell, his washing of his hands of him. Like Hugh Medairy he was vanishing before Val Sturgis' eyes, and Val Sturgis was already moving to a world Harold had once hoped to reach but had lost and then abandoned.

They embraced a long time at the door.

Coming back into the empty room, Val looked down at the sheets of music his teacher had brought to him.

"Everything in my life is a succession of goodbyes," Val said. He looked over at the piano. He picked up one of the imported bon-bons from Mr. Vane and let it melt on his tongue.

Then he sat down at the piano and let his hands crash down on the keys. His head fell over his hands. He was too hurt to weep.

It was still dark out when Val got up off the mattress on the floor and began to brew coffee. He felt a hundred years had gone by since Harold had given his goodbye, since Hugh Medairy had given his. He tried to eat his piece of slightly overdone toast, but it turned his stomach. He was about to go out for a walk when the intercom sounded. Ezekiel Loomis' calm firm voice resonated in the room. He would be coming right up.

A whole avalanche of thoughts came to the composer. He was positive Ezekiel was bringing another notice of termination.

Waiting for the servant, Val looked out the window. The sun had risen, engulfed in purple and black clouds.

Ezekiel refused any refreshment, and Val felt his refusal boded ill.

"Mr. Blossom would like you to come for lunch at half past one today."

Val nodded his acceptance.

Ezekiel hesitated to say more and Val was too frightened to encourage him to explain the urgency of his being summoned to the Hotel Enrique. But finally unable to keep silent, Val blurted out: "Ezekiel, why don't you tell me what this is really all about."

Ezekiel sat down. He refused Val's second offer of refreshment. "Mr. Blossom will explain it all so much better than I can," Ezekiel hedged.

Val also sat down and went on drinking his morning brew. "Is it the Reszkes, Ezekiel?" Val raised his voice.

"Of course."

"And is Abner angry with me?"

Ezekiel looked genuinely surprised. "Angry with you? Of course not. With them he is furious though."

Val Sturgis almost dissolved before the servant in this sudden reprieve. "Tell Mr. Blossom I'll be there on time."

The day after all turned out to be a fine one, and Val decided to walk all the way from his flat on Grove Street to the Chelsea district and the Hotel Enrique.

> "They go, they come,
> like apple blossoms"

He hummed the words from one of his old songs.

He had dressed carefully, formally, punctiliously for the occasion.

He remembered all at once having so often complained to

Hugh Medairy that he had never been invited to one of Abner Blossom's famous banquets at the Enrique, and he remembered now what Hugh Medairy had said in reply:

"Abner Blossom though invites you to something more prestigious, his luncheons with you and you alone where the old maestro gives you more attention and encouragement than at a hundred of his banquets. . . ."

Still humming one of his own songs, Val bought a flower for his buttonhole from a young street vendor, who after receiving Val's fifty-cent piece cried out, "Good luck, sir."

Abner Blossom was seated in his private study. He did not rise as Val Sturgis entered.

"Over there, where I can see you better," Abner said in a loud but not unfriendly manner, but one short of cordiality. Abner continued to look at a long foolscap page, as if he were going over the various derelictions and shortcomings of his disciple.

A single fat tear escaped from Val's right eye as he thought for some reason again on his never being invited to the banquets at Abner's where all the famous assembled at least once a week.

"Did you flirt with Harold Reszke?" came the first question.

Before Val could reply Ezekiel brought in the refreshment which today was grilled ham and cheese sandwiches but which Abner took pains to describe as one of his French specialties, *croque monsieur*. Val took a bite of the *croque monsieur* and chewed appreciatively.

"No, sir, I did not."

"You never cast sheep's eyes at him?" the judge pursued the inquiry.

"I was too in awe of him to do so."

"Good," Abner's eyes returned to the foolscap.

"No over zealous pressures on your teacher, no holding his hand overlong when saying goodbye or hello, no batting of your eyelashes to show love-sickness?"

Val tried to control his temper now, and so instead of saying any more, he merely shook his head vigorously.

Putting aside the foolscap and tasting his *croque monsieur*,

Abner Blossom went into a kind of reverie.

"I knew the Reszkes in Paris of course, ten years ago, when Harold was attempting a kind of modest success with his piano solos, but even then Laetitia guarded him like a lioness her cub. At that time Harold had not lost the use of his leg (he was injured in a skiing accident I believe) and so he could run about the *trottoirs* free of his wife. But when he became a cripple, Laetitia's jealousy of him grew even more enormously, if you can imagine jealousy like hers being able to increase in intensity. She is only jealous of men, young men especially, that is, and it turns out she is especially so of you. She fears you as if you were time's end."

Abner rang the bell for Ezekiel who was stationed conveniently by the door, and who now entered and removed the dishes.

"Then you swear, dear Val, you are innocent?" Abner brought his interrogatory forward.

"It never crossed my mind, dear Abner, to flirt with a teacher like Reszke." Here Val gazed somewhat piteously at Ezekiel who had put down before him a finger bowl in which a piece of lemon swam. Val touched only the edge of the bowl. "I have never been accused of such a thing," he added brokenly.

"You are through at their house, innocent or guilty, Val. It's me however who has been put on trial by that harpy. She was here, as Ezekiel can testify." And here the composer with a flourish of his right hand waved away his servant.

Val could spy Ezekiel a moment later hiding behind a crack in the oak door and quietly listening but not so quietly snickering.

"She broke in here last night." Abner now recounted the details of the outrage. "Nearly knocked Ezekiel down, rushed directly into my bedroom where I was about to put out the light. She called me a strong pejorative in French, for she pretends she knows French better than English which as a matter of fact may be correct since she knows neither language. They're Polish, these Reszkes or so they claim, but one thing is for sure: they are impostors, at least she is. Even Harold's own musical output is highly suspect in my opinion."

"But he has talent, certainly, Abner."

"Are you putting words into my mouth?" Abner's anger now came out clearly. It was obvious he was smarting terribly from Laetitia's run-in with him.

"She accused me, our Laetitia, of sending you to Harold in order to entrap him, to have an affair with him, to, in short, take him away from her, and force him to join the world of what she denominates the empire of pederasty of which she says I am the ringleader. She threw in my face that I have ruined more young men than the Marquis de Sade. . . ."

Val Sturgis was slowly sinking into an even deeper depression at hearing of Laetitia's invasion, and he understood now why Harold had broken off their relationship. At the same time he couldn't help being amused by hearing Ezekiel's snickering coming from behind the door. It was a good thing perhaps Abner's hearing was no longer keen.

"Now, now, Val," Abner spoke consolingly as he saw what he thought was a tear coming down the young composer's cheek. "You are excused. I know, I can size it up. Laetitia on leaving, however, broke my prize antique, my great-grandmother's china closet. She threw a paperweight against it. . . . But I accept the fact you did not flirt with her precious Harold, did not press his hand too tightly (you have a firm grip I must concede), and did not gaze at his fly with absorption. No, you are exonerated. And I herewith wash my hands of the Reszkes. I could have helped them both, helped Harold inordinately. I offered many a time to introduce him to Metropolis, and others, who would look over his four or five symphonies. . . ."

Val began to come out of his blues.

Abner went on. "But Harold is prouder than the highest Himalayas. He is above us all, reigns already in his own paradise, but all the same he dwells below, caged by his tigerish spouse whose claws and fangs grow longer and sharper by the day. And meanwhile goodbye to my china closet."

Abner now stood up indicating the session was nearing its end. Val's mouth opened rather wide as he realized Abner's height was hardly more pronounced standing than sitting, at least it seemed so then to him.

Val also rose, brushing off some crumbs from his jacket.

"I will try to find another teacher for you, Val. Though I am pleased to say Harold complimented you rather grandly for what you are composing, pity. He would have been a perfect teacher for you, I will not belittle his gift there!"

As Abner was shaking hands goodbye with his disciple, he whispered "Did you not think Harold fetching though?"

Another tear came down Val's cheek, as Ezekiel opened the door for him and softly said, "Good day, young man, and good luck too."

Val Sturgis' grandmother who had raised him in a small town in Kentucky had often consoled her grandson with the saying "When God closes one door he opens another."

Perhaps he thought of her words when a few days after his session at the Hotel Enrique with Abner Blossom, a new door did indeed open unexpectedly. The front door bell had been ringing vigorously for some time.

Hurrying out wearing only his dressing gown, Val saw a tall blond man with side-whiskers with a kind of doorman's long coat and garrison hat, and bearing a large stiff envelope.

"Mr. Valentine Sturgis?" the man inquired in a bored, irritable voice.

Val nodded.

"I have something for you to sign and then I need your written reply to this," and he displayed the envelope he was carrying.

"Will you come in, please," Val tightened the cord on his dressing gown, and looked embarrassedly down at his bare feet.

Inside Val invited the caller to sit down while he opened the document. It read:

"I have unfortunately missed seeing you the times you came to my husband's photography studio. I have heard of your talent from Mr. Abner Blossom, among others, and I wish to invite you to my private table at the Rumpelkammer restaurant today at 2.0 p.m. Please give the messenger, Claude Bingham, your reply, as I can trust him implicitly. (I do not trust Harlan Yost, my husband's secretary, with any messages of importance: bear this in mind for the future.)

I will await you then at Rumpelkammer's. Remember, I do not take No for an answer,

Olga Petrovna

Val put down the thick document-like message with considerable perplexity and worry. He observed the messenger, Claude Bingham, was helping himself to Cyril Vane's gift of imported bon-bons and chewing loudly.

"Well, here goes another cancellation I guess at Elena Baclanova's," Val began.

Claude Bingham had removed his garrison cap and stared at the composer with a look of total contempt.

"You can't seriously compare Olga Petrovna with Elena Baclanova now, can you?"

"And why ever not," Val replied heatedly. "Everyone in the world knows the name of the diva Baclanova, while nobody –"

"Wait a minute," Claude replied just as heatedly. "Granted your diva Baclanova may have enjoyed her fame at the Opera, that is, on the days she felt like singing, but what does Miss Baclanova have today, may I ask you? Certainly not money. I doubt she pays you enough for your subway fare and a slice of pizza. Everyone knows Miss Baclanova spent all she ever earned on her many young male lovers. Now look at the position Miss Petrovna occupies. She can dip at any hour into the pot of gold reserved for her at Mr. Cyril Vane's and no questions asked. If you wish to rise in the world forget Miss Baclanova, at least when you have nothing better to do, and give your prime attention to Miss Petrovna. I know whereof I speak."

Claude Bingham then rose and put on his garrison cap sideways and grimaced at the astounded composer.

"You wouldn't have some spirits around the house, would you?" the messenger inquired as he placed the document to be signed within reach of Val Sturgis' clasped hands.

"Yes, you'll find several bottles on the kitchen table," Val spoke in a whisper while staring at the document he was supposed to sign.

"Ah, what good taste somebody has," Claude commented inspecting the labels on the bottles and then pouring himself a generous shot of brandy.

"Haven't you signed yet, Val Sturgis," the messenger began scolding again as he looked over the composer's shoulder. "May I say something more?" Claude went on as he saw Val sign the paper now. "Anybody keeping the fast company you have obviously been keeping should not worry one second about breaking his date with Diva Baclanova. As the old saw has it, she needs you more than you need her. Wake up to your future, young man. Wake up to opportunity, not piano and voice lessons!"

Saying this, the messenger seized the signed document, read it again and gave out a pleased guffaw. "Right, right," he chirped and downed his glass of brandy. After this impudent speech, Claude Bingham gave the composer a rough embrace, adjusted his garrison hat to the proper angle, and walked to the door brandishing the signed acceptance paper in a kind of farewell flourish.

"Rumpelkammer's then!" Claude Bingham shouted with forced gaiety. "And don't be late."

Val muttered some inaudible words of farewell as the messenger closed the door behind him. He sighed deeply. He was positive at that moment that he had lost his position as accompanist to Elena Baclanova.

Going by foot to Rumpelkammer's, Val Sturgis thought he could hear again the angry voice of Abner Blossom who, on being told that Val was going to see Olga Petrovna, had cried,

"Don't be a bigger fool than you are! Don't you understand that by seeing her you will sour your friendship with Cyril Vane. Have you no sense of proportion?"

Val had all but hung up on Abner. "Everything I do is wrong," he thought and then stopped to look at himself in one of the showcase windows along Fifth Avenue. He straightened his tie which he had borrowed from Hugh Medairy, and wiped a bit of soot from his cheek.

"Don't go, whatever you do, do not see her!" Abner's words came back in memory all the way to Central Park South.

Val was on his way to Rumpelkammer's a little early as one of his many failings was his tendency to arrive late (his memory of being fired from the chorus of the Metropolitan Opera never left him). He stood for a few seconds now before the ornate gilt splendor of Rumpelkammer's and suddenly almost lost his nerve. He thought of catching a cab and going home.

In the midst of his hesitation he felt a strong hand laid on his shoulder. A familiar if slightly changed voice called his name. He looked up to see Harold Reszke. Taking his pupil's hand, Harold mumbled a few worn phrases, and then speaking in his old regal manner said:

"Let's step over here to this little bar, why don't we."

Val took a long look now at Harold. He was greatly changed, and badly wanted a shave. His eyes were haggard and the clothes he had on were not suitable for this part of town.

Inside the tiny bar, Harold smiled broadly at the pleasure of seeing his pupil again. He clapped his hands in the European style, and a waiter appeared at once and addressed the teacher familiarly. Without consulting Val Harold ordered two glasses of a wine with a long name.

"And what are you doing in this neighborhood?" Harold wondered when the wine had been served and he was tasting it loudly.

Val hesitated a moment before saying: "I have an appointment with Olga Petrovna."

Harold banged down his glass and gave his pupil a look of savage reproach. Then shaking his head ruefully, he said: "Well, what will be, will be," and raised his glass and drank thirstily.

Then shaking his head again and again he added: "Oh, well, Val, who am I to criticize anybody."

Harold sipped now suspiciously at his wine as if the waiter had brought the wrong kind.

"If I were only the man I was in Paris, how different things would be," he reflected. "And if I were not dependent on this," he picked up his crutch and banged it against the table. "Let me tell you what I would do! For one thing I would take you in hand, and you would be the composer of the hour!"

He grasped his crutch tightly now and brought it closer to the table. "You are still composing I hope," he raised his voice.

"All the time, all the time."

Harold smiled sadly. At a signal from the teacher the waiter had brought two more glasses of wine.

"I must be going, Harold. I am already late. Really and truly."

"If I were only free," the teacher went on as if he had not heard. Then: "Don't ever marry, my friend," Harold turned now to give Val an eloquent look such as the song writer felt he had never seen on any face before. "Be free, be alone, and work."

Harold rose now without the aid of his crutch and Val also got up not having touched his second glass.

"What does anything matter but *it*. If we were only in Paris together, and I was free. Go on now to your appointment, go ahead. But remember. . . ." Harold slumped down in his chair and took hold of his crutch. "I send you every heartfelt wish for your career." He seemed to speak to the second glass of wine. "Goodbye, Val, go to your lady."

Val Sturgis shook his teacher's hand and then hurried out.

"I knew you'd be late," Olga Petrovna said, putting down her lorgnette, heavy with sparkling gems of some indefinable sort. "So I didn't wait." She raised her glass. "Your mouth is stained," she observed, and handed Val a napkin.

"Could you believe it, Mrs. Vane," Val began, "I ran into my former composition and harmony teacher."

"Why do you need a teacher when my husband says you are a supreme talent?"

"One of my critics said I have more pizzaz than genius."

"Ah, well, critics," she shrugged. "In my day in films, I was either compared to Duse or burned at the stake. Thank God anyhow you came. I thought as I was being sped over here perilously in a taxi where the driver spoke no known language, I thought, what will we say to one another. And *say*, dear young man, we must."

Suddenly Val wiped away a tear. Olga handed him now her own handkerchief and then asked the waiter to fetch two more napkins.

"I knew the minute I set eyes on you, may I call you Val, I knew, Val the day you entered Cyril's drawing room for it is *his*, don't you see, not mine. I knew I say, you were a find! I am a kind of life-term guest like an aunt or a mother to my husband, though I married Cyril nearly fifty years ago. Don't say it, don't say it, that I don't look that old. I feel a hundred, oh give it two hundred. Like the woman She in an old Victorian romance. But when you came, I thought perhaps the world could change. Perhaps Cyril will begin to see *human* young men who come from families and background, and don't have rings in their nose. You have no idea the position I occupy there. But do you think he would give me up. I've asked him since the last forty years to allow me to divorce him. All he does is smile in reply (those smiles so reminiscent of the laughing cobra) then he takes me in his arms and kisses me till I am the consistency of jelly. I am not allowed in the studio. I am indeed a prisoner. But I have grown accustomed to humiliation." Here Olga beckoned the waiter to refill her glass. Val felt some small reassurance when he saw she was drinking merely sweet cider.

"I never touch alcohol, nor smoke, and was born too early for drugs," Olga explained. "Cyril tries to get me to take snuff. And the snuff comes from one of his amours, Nita Naldi. You won't have heard of her I suppose. I must always remind myself

I am yesterday. Listen, I adore you. Will you be my friend? Of course, you can go on seeing Cyril until he tires of you. Listen. He tires of everybody. I am kept, in irons, only for one reason, I've decided. I am hopeless, irretrievable. I know everything about him except the details in the studio, and I remind him that he has had a past. That I am his past, for in my case the *now* merges imperceptibly into the *then*.

"I love you," Olga told Val. "Adore you." She took out her compact and powdered her cheeks and chin, and some of the powder flew into Val's nose causing him to sneeze.

"But enough of me and mine, dear young man. Enough of the past! It's what's going on today and will happen tomorrow that concerns me. You can help me. At least allay my fears, or at least confirm them. Listen well, Val Sturgis. Lean a bit closer so that we are not overheard. Good. What a wonderful smelling hair-dressing you have on. Listen well, my dear. Is it a fact" (and here Olga Petrovna put her mouth firmly against Val's right ear) "is what they are whispering true? That Abner Blossom is writing an opera based on me and Cyril Vane. Oh tell the truth even if it kills me and I fall dead at your feet. Don't spare me. I must have the truth. I cannot abide suspense. Of all human suffering it is the most unendurable. So, dear wonderful young talent! Speak!"

For once in his life Val Sturgis was able to defend Abner Blossom by shamefacedly lying, prevaricating, for by so doing he was certain he was protecting his mentor and guide and, who knows, putting to rest the fears of this renowned actress of the silver and silent screen.

"There is not a word of truth in it," Val spoke brazenly and just as brazenly stared into Olga's eyes.

She fished out her lorgnette and stared back at his eyes.

"Either you are the most disingenuous of young men, my dear, or else you are the most consummate liar who ever drew breath! Which are you? Speak!"

"Abner Blossom has told me not once but again and again, dear lady, he never writes about real or living people."

"Oh thank God, thank God. Let me embrace you." Olga rose and threw her arms about her guest. "You have absolutely destroyed all suspense, all suspicion. I am a free woman again, dear Val. Free and all due to you. You have released me from bondage, weeks of pain, insomnia, and terror."

Silent briefly, Olga then went on, "I reached America people will tell you on a cattle boat with Alla Nazimova. We were met at the boat by a great impressario. We were both kidnapped according to the story and after having been deflowered by gladiators, were given parts in a Broadway musical. All lies of course. I only knew Nazimova one might say socially, though my husband was smitten with her in the days when women were part of his rigamarole. But you are different." Here Olga clapped her hands even more forcibly than Harold had, and a dignified man in what looked almost like full military uniform approached the table, bowing almost to his knees.

"Is the piano ready?" Olga inquired raising but not looking through her lorgnette.

"It is awaiting your pleasure, kind Madame Petrovna."

"This young gentleman will play for us."

"But Madame Petrovna," Val began, "I am a composer, not a pianist."

"Who ever heard of a composer who could not play the piano. Don't humiliate all of us with such folderol. Get on that stool yonder and Play."

Val had drunk enough by then not to fear ruin or shame. He sat down. He looked back at Madame Petrovna who was strangely enough powdering part of her exposed bosom with a large powder puff. Catching sight of Val's troubled gaze, she cried:

"Let us hear all of the eighty-eight keys, my darling."

Val played, applause began to filter through from the adjoining rooms, and it cheered him on. He played until another major-domo of sorts came bearing a message from Madame Petrovna. Val realized without reading the message his hostess had heard him, and gone.

"I am torn between this great person and that!" Val spoke aloud to himself. Olga and Rumpelkammer's seemed far away, even forgotten. Instead of taking the subway home to his Grove Street rooms, he walked. It began to rain. He hardly noticed it. He was thinking how great people had suddenly taken him on, but that each one required a different thing from him, and one different thing did not jibe or blend with what the other party required of him. He could please one and displease the others, or even if he pleased only one, that one person might at some time turn angry, become dissatisfied and banish him. He saw banishment as inevitable. He wanted to stay close to Abner Blossom, but he was aware of how many disciples before him had been shut out one day in the dark, and never allowed to appear in his studio again. And though Cyril Vane was no longer esteemed as a name in the world, his past grandeur made Val want to serve him also, be welcomed to his dark-room, be photographed and praised for what Vane called his 1880 musical genius. And finally there was his exiled fluttering wife, Olga Petrovna of the silent screen, promising Val he could find sustenance, inspiration, and true acclaim if he joined her circle.

In the rain he could hear again Abner's voice forbidding him to know Olga Petrovna, forbidding him, actually, to have much to do even with Cyril. "Let him photograph you, yes, you may even give yourself to him, but let it end there. Do you hear, let it end there!" Abner's high treble voice reached through the rain drops, saying: "But Olga Petrovna, god alive, never! Do you want to go back into the silent screen with her, and become a lotus-eater. Olga Petrovna has ruined nearly all of Cyril's lovers, once she beckons them away from him."

One of Val's most annoying habits from the point of view of his worldly friends was, as we have noted previously, his ability to weep like a young damsel in distress. Tormented by these reflections, Val stood in a doorway near Sixth Avenue and began to cry in earnest. He felt old, all at once, at twenty-five. He felt orphaned and lost, and unsure of his own talent even though important persons had been praising that talent to the skies. He heard again Abner in one of his more acerbic moments cry: "Beware of praise. It is rat poison."

Val gradually became aware of a young man with shoulder-length curly hair eyeing him from a doorway protected from the downpour. Val gave him a faint welcoming smile. He did not need to smile again. The young man pulled out a worn, extremely large umbrella from where it had been resting near the doorway and stepped over to the composer.

"Why you're sopping wet," the newcomer observed. "Better get under my umbrella, why don't you."

As he raised the umbrella over Val, Val noticed a ring of expensive gold on his right hand. The young man noticed Val's eyes on the ring, and smiling he held his hand closer to Val as if he were a jewel merchant showing his ware. As they stood together under the umbrella the newcomer said "My name is Luigi Cervo."

"Since we have your umbrella, Luigi," Val said, "let's go over to my place nearby."

Luigi nodded agreement and the two began hurrying through the downpour which had now increased in volume to a real cloudburst.

Val's hand shook so much as he tried to put his key in the lock to his apartment that Luigi finally took the key in his hand and opened the door.

"My hands are not as cold as yours," Luigi joked as they entered the flat.

Val half-expected to find Hugh Medairy waiting in the room as they entered. When Val turned on all the overhead lights, the remembrance of Hugh made him feel a sudden pulse of sickness.

Looking up he saw Luigi observing him closely.

"We should put on some dry clothes," Val spoke up now coming out of his feelings which were as turbulent as the downpour outside.

Luigi smiled his strange expressive smile. Val noticed a small jagged white scar above the young man's right eyebrow, and another smaller scar across his chin.

Val walked over to one of the large back closets, and brought out two oversize bathrobes. Almost tearing the better looking robe out of Val's hands, Luigi stepped quickly out of all his clothes like a veteran acrobat in a carnival, and then hugged himself into the billowing dressing gown.

"I like the smell and feel of this robe," Luigi said. As he pressed his hands against the buttons of the robe, his gold ring sparkled in the light.

Val more decorously undressed, his back to his visitor, and stepped into his dressing gown which now all at once gave out a strong smell of camphor.

"Could you make us something hot, do you think?" Luigi inquired, and he sat down all at once in the large armchair in which Hugh Medairy had used to study his music for the Men's Chorus.

"Do you have coffee?" Luigi asked when Val did not reply at once.

Val nodded.

"Could I make it?"

As if Luigi sensed his host was probably the world's worst cook, Val had soon shown the newcomer where everything was waiting for the preparation of the drink. To Val's surprise, his new friend in no time at all had made from the few things available in the kitchen two cups of steaming hot capuccino.

Taking his own cup, Luigi drank his coffee lying back on a large divan which Val had found one day abandoned outside a fashionable brownstone.

Val studied his new friend who was savoring greedily the taste of his hot drink. The sudden sight of Luigi's exposed left nipple appearing almost black in the subdued light of the room, drew the composer nearer. Again Luigi appeared to be purposely holding up his hand with the resplendent ring.

"And what might your name be?" Luigi spoke sombrely. Apologising for this omission Val told him.

"Excuse me, Luigi, but is that beautiful ring you're wearing possibly a keepsake from your family?"

"Keepsake?" Luigi straightened up now from his former reclining position on the divan. Thinking gloomily for a moment, Luigi replied, "I wouldn't exactly call it that, no."

"You look at the ring every so often, that's all I mean."

"Val," Luigi began setting down his coffee, and looking fixedly at Val. "Who moved out on you here?"

"Oh, well," Val looked down at his bare feet.

"If you don't want to tell me, don't."

"It was a close friend of mine," Val muttered. "We were together for some years."

"I figured something like that," Luigi said and rose now. His eye for the first time rested on the sight of the piano shrouded in the interior of the apartment. He walked directly over to it and played a few chords. Then perhaps liking the sound he sat down on the piano stool and, singing, let out a cascade of dulcet baritone notes.

The sound of Luigi's voice even more than the handsomeness of his person melted the composer. He came over to where Luigi was sitting and touched Luigi's right hand resting on the keys.

"If I play something, Luigi, will you sing?"

Luigi rose from the piano stool and Val began playing one of his own compositions.

Had a nightingale or a lark flown into the room, Val would later tell Abner Blossom, he could not have been more moved. Together they played and sang on into the morning hours.

As the last of the songs died away, Luigi bent down and solemnly kissed the composer, and then curiously put his right index finger almost painfully on the composer's nostrils.

Turning to face the singer, Val felt Luigi's cool lips against his own, pressing almost painfully against his teeth.

"Val," Luigi said, and held him against his chest, "thank fortune for the downpour, don't you say?"

The night after Olga's meeting with Val Sturgis happened to be opera night for the Vanes. Long a patron of grand opera, over the last few years Cyril and Olga had taken advantage of their attendance in the choicest box the house offered to settle their many grievances and complaints with one another. Tonight was to be no exception.

Olga Petrovna feared constantly that Cyril Vane had her watched, or in her phrase "shadowed" by detectives. What had aroused this suspicion was her having once heard her husband conferring with a famous detective in the study adjoining the dark-room. What Olga had not realized however was the detective was investigating one of Cyril's photographic models, a young black man who had escaped from a chain gang in Alabama.

At the same time Olga felt her suspicions as to being shadowed were slightly improbable. Cyril Vane was too close with his money to hire a detective for *her*. And then she might have remembered from bitter past experiences that Cyril need not have gone to the expense of a private eye: his many young friends, most of whom were models, would invariably report to him Olga's comings and goings.

And tonight in the tinsel grandeur of the opera house Olga, after close study of her husband's manner, realized someone had tattled and told him she had met privately with Val Sturgis.

During the opera, Cyril's face was wreathed in smiles, always a sign trouble was brewing. He was, she saw, spoiling for a good fight with her, and the opera house had always been for both of them a favorite site for quarreling.

For the Vanes went to the opera much as some Catholics go to mass, attendant only in body. And Cyril had said a thousand times he had seen all the great singers, and there was nobody any more who truly interested him since the days of Mary Garden. Yes, he must have been thinking (Olga was sure) that there was no better place for a squabble than where they sat enthroned regally.

The overture to tonight's opera had hardly begun when Cyril touching his wife's naked elbow said sweetly, "Did you enjoy the pudding at Rumpelkammer's yesterday, my dear?"

Olga opened her mouth in a deadly smile.

"*Pudding* at Rumpelkammer's?" she finally inquired.

"And how many charlotte russes did you consume?" he wondered and gave a coy look at her abdomen.

Olga pretended to be livid with rage in line with her past

behavior at these domestic tempests. She sputtered some faint insults but purposely uttered far from his good ear.

A woman seated a few boxes away whispered "Shh," and tapped her fan against her program.

"I have no life of my own, no privacy, no place to go without being hounded and spied upon, listened to and carefully recorded even when as yesterday there was a thunderstorm."

Cyril handed her a fresh handkerchief which she accepted languidly and dabbed her eyes.

"Val Sturgis may seem an easy target, my dear," Cyril carefully eyed a new diamond brooch he had not seen previously on his wife's bosom, "but see here, even a young relocated hillbilly like Mr. Sturgis knows your only interest in him is to get back at me!"

Olga made a motion to rise, but Cyril took her ermine coat and held it firmly away from her reach.

"Will you please be quiet?" a male voice from a nearby box pleaded.

But all at once something changed between the two contestants. Olga dropped her role as injured wife, loveless spouse, abused Griselda followed by imaginary detectives. She looked carefully almost compassionately at her husband.

She had noticed for some time that Cyril was failing. Even their quarrels as tonight lacked style and vigor and could not be compared with the free-for-alls of their prime. Their quarrels now resembled those of tired actors reading from a hastily perused script.

The thought of Cyril dying, leaving her was as impossible to credit as if all the eastern seaboard of North America was to quake and go under the sea.

Olga often attempted to tune in to his own private meditations. Cyril enjoyed everything now so appreciatively as one who examines the face of a loved one who is leaving for a long sea journey. Cyril, she felt, was saying goodbye to all things dear to him, all persons close to his heart. Olga therefore welcomed their tiffs and spats as it took her mind off death and endless oblivion.

"You cannot, you shall not have Val Sturgis," Cyril

warned her. "Besides, he belongs to Abner Blossom."

Shrugging aside her gloomy thoughts of death and parting, Olga warmed to the fray. The fight was on.

"Oh merciful God," Olga cried out in her old termagant manner, for the name of Abner Blossom always struck a painful chord.

A cloud of fear and exasperation came over her countenance as she heard the old composer's name. A few years ago, even a few months ago Olga would have told Cyril she had information that Abner Blossom was writing an opera based on their lives. It was now all she could do to restrain her tongue from revealing a secret which tormented her almost as much as Cyril's failing health. She kept silent by sheer willpower.

It was Cyril's turn to be disturbed by the expression of anguish on his wife's face.

Seeing he was aware something unknown to him was tormenting her, Olga launched into a tirade against Abner Blossom and his circle of over-civilized young men.

Cyril listened patiently as Olga abused the old composer, disparaged his banquets, and his harem of young men.

As the fray diminished then in fury and volume, Olga touched Cyril's arm, and spoke almost beatifically.

"Your Mr. Sturgis plays so beautifully, sweet," she muttered in his good ear. "Cyril, you are right to love him, your Mr. Sturgis."

"Love him?" Cyril raised his voice in mock outrage. "Have you lost the last of your wits, misguided love?"

She knew she had hit a nerve, and smiled. She reflected then all the while smiling that smile which had always infuriated him even when he had been courting her. Olga Petrovna knew and did not know what went on in the dark-room of Cyril's suite of rooms. But always as tonight during heated arguments Olga would let fall phrases and oblique comments which both seemed to reveal her complete knowledge of his secret life and also oddly enough appeared to be excuses for his proclivities, just as a doting mother will brush away the knowledge that her favorite child is a sneak thief.

Olga would often wake up in a sweat in the middle of

slumber with the thought that her husband might at that very moment in the dark-room be gaining life energy by caressing the fountainhead of some young black man's spring source.

Seeing she was sunk into some meditation of her own, Cyril surrendered back her coat and let it fall over her lap, and then taking her left hand in his, held it painfully tight. She wept silently now nodding under his sudden kindness, and then – fell sound asleep. Cyril followed suit a few minutes later.

As they were perhaps the most lavish patrons of the opera, they felt rightly they were in its precincts merely at home. And then to look around from their box, to see so many empty seats everywhere, one felt the singers were giving a command performance solely for the Vanes, even when as now they took a brief nap.

No honeymoon, Val Sturgis was much later to describe it, yes, no honeymoon could ever have been so blissful. Those few short weeks with Luigi were the only blissful days of his life. He had never before been happy, never even before been at peace.

Still "honeymoon" was not a word he cared for. It was for the common herd, a word used by suburban shoppers and reporters.

But as the days and weeks passed, Val became apprehensive and more nervous than ever, and in the midst of his joy a presentiment of loss and sorrow was always present.

"What's amiss?" Luigi Cervo would often inquire worriedly as he studied his friend. "Tell me, what's troubling you?"

In the evening even when the weather was bad they took long strolls through the Village.

One evening as they were promenading, laughing like schoolboys, staring in expensive shop-windows, Val caught a sudden sight of Cyril Vane and his assistant Harlan Yost seated in one of the more expensive outdoor cafes. Val grasped hold of

Luigi and pulled him away from the proximity of Cyril Vane, but Cyril had already caught sight of them and sent Harlan Yost rushing after the pair.

"What's your rush, gentlemen," Harlan Yost was all smiles but there was a trace of temper and sour reproof in his tone.

While Val babbled some excuses, Yost took the composer by the hand and looking in Luigi's direction, said "Mr. Vane wants both of you to join his table. Please be sensible," he added.

Val's heart gave a twinge when they had seated themselves with the photographer. The old man was studying Luigi intently as one would pour over a map in a guidebook. Cyril paid no more attention to Val from that moment on.

"An incredible face," Cyril whispered to Harlan Yost. "I have seldom seen anything to equal it."

As they all sipped their frosted pineapple drinks heavy on rum and brandy, a concoction which the bartender made only for Cyril Vane, the photographer now turned to Val and said in an uncivil tone:

"What on earth possessed you to run away from us tonight like a streak of lightning?"

Val saw the photographer was perhaps picking a fight with him so that he could disguise his extreme admiration of Luigi. He began offering some mumbled excuses, but Cyril Vane was going on: "I don't like being snubbed, do I, Harlan."

Harlan nodded and drank deeply from his pineapple sling.

"No, Mr. Vane doesn't like rudeness," the assistant finally volunteered.

To Val's extreme discomfort, Mr. Vane lapsed into silence, lost in wonder at what he would later call the spectacle of Luigi's pulchritude.

Val had the impression he was in the throes of some frightful but long-anticipated nightmare. Mr. Vane's next comment added to his foreboding.

"I would like to ask your friend, Val, to come to the studio tomorrow night, if you have no objection, for a photography session. We do not have anything scheduled tomorrow, do we?" Cyril now inquired of Harlan Yost.

The assistant confirmed they were free.

"You need not come, Val, unless of course you wish to renew your acquaintance with my wife. I understand you and Olga had a delightful afternoon at Rumpelkammer's the other day."

Val caught a sardonic smile on Harlan Yost's face.

It was all too clear to Val at that moment that he had fallen from the good graces of Mr. Vane perhaps by reason of his rendezvous with Olga Petrovna. Or perhaps Mr. Vane was displeased merely by the fact that Val was friend to Luigi whom later Mr. Vane was to call the Antinous of our day. What grieved Val more than anything else however was the fact that his Luigi was all too clearly eager to visit the photographer's studio.

Mr. Vane and Luigi now began speaking together, joking and laughing as if they were old acquaintances who had by chance run into one another after a lapse of time. Both Val Sturgis and Harlan Yost found themselves left out of the conversation as if they were seated at a separate table.

As the pineapple slings were reordered again and again and Mr. Vane made no effort to bring Val or Harlan into his private tête-à-tête with Luigi Cervo, a curtain of gloom fell over Val. He ignored the few attempts by Harlan Yost to enter into conversation. He sat isolated and silent now as if he were seated alone. He also found he was unable to control his eyes from watering and his mouth from trembling with sorrow and rising anger.

Finally even Mr. Vane became aware of the change in the atmosphere. He made a few lame attempts to bring back Val into the conversation. Unable to endure it any longer, Val suddenly sprang up and announced that he would have to be leaving.

Coming out of his own absorption with the brilliant repartee of Mr. Vane, Luigi pushed aside his drink and rose also. He sensed at that moment his friend's pain and chagrin.

"Val," he said softly. "What is it?"

Luigi's obvious concern caused Val to sob audibly, and he turned away from everyone at the table, and without bothering to say goodnight, began walking away from the cafe.

Luigi made a few hurried excuses to Mr. Vane and Harlan and hurried after his friend.

At first Val broke away from Luigi's putting his arm around him.

Then Luigi's own anger burst: "What are you doing to me?" he shouted, attracting the attention of a group of young men who had been observing them.

"Leave me alone," Val managed to speak at last.

"What are you carrying on like this for, Val? You're certainly not jealous of a tottering old man like Mr. Vane. Who after all is a friend of yours, not mine."

"I don't want to talk about it. You've made your appointment with him. So go tomorrow, don't worry about me."

"You know damned well I worry about you," Luigi broke now into real anger.

It was at that moment that both young men realized how deeply they needed one another.

Val threw himself into Luigi's arms. Standing together in embrace, they were oblivious to the fact a small crowd had gathered round them, some of whom jeered and called them names. They were oblivious to everything just then but their need of one another's love.

Back in their flat, Luigi prepared some jasmine tea for his friend, and coaxed him back into good humor.

"I won't go if you feel this way," Luigi spoke after they had sat in happy silence, the tea untouched and growing cold.

"No, no, I won't allow you to break your engagement with him," Val protested. "Besides you'll have wonderful photos, some of which I hope I can possess also."

"You possess me," Luigi said thickly. "Can you think for a moment Mr. Vane could mean anything to me after I have found you."

Even Luigi appeared on the point of tears.

Val's eyes rested then on the gold ring as if it too were some sort of warning and threat.

Luigi all at once removed the ring. "Why don't you take it, Val. I know it worries you. Take it."

Val protested and Luigi put it back on his finger.

"I will tell you about it one day. Give me some time yet, and I'll tell you everything."

Luigi had no more said goodbye to Valentine Sturgis the next evening prior to his going to Cyril Vane's studio than the composer, on closing the door on his friend, felt an overpowering sickness almost as if he had accidentally mistaken poison for water. He lay down, with a burning sensation on his tongue and a throbbing in both his temples.

He realized then he had fallen hopelessly in love with Luigi. And though he knew next to nothing about his friend, Val felt they had been together for years, almost from boyhood. Had Hugh Medairy received an invitation to go to Cyril Vane's studio alone for additional photos, Val would have felt no particular emotion at all, certainly no jealousy. He had loved Hugh but only as one loves a brother or a member of his family. But Luigi in the short time they had been together was a fire in his veins. Besides the handsomeness of his person Luigi was gifted in many ways – at home both in Italian and English, and a singer of talent. Although a few years younger than Val, he could quote from Dante and Petrarch and the *Sonnets* of Shakespeare for hours on end. Luigi was surprised at Val's own lack of education, and once said acidly, "I guess all you know is composing." To make up for this remark he then kissed Val tenderly.

But in a painful reflective mood, Val began to realize he knew nothing about Luigi Cervo. There was something mysterious about Luigi's materialization in that downpour, without possessions or identification, and always there was some noticeable deep sadness and hurt in Luigi which only made his physical beauty more alluring.

The realization kept coming again and again that though Val was hopelessly in love with Luigi, he was positive that Luigi did not feel as strongly for him. Luigi loved him of course, but not in the overmastering way Val loved him.

In his turmoil, Val walked the streets. All at once he found himself in front of the decayed Victorian grandeur of the Hotel Enrique. He decided he would risk calling on Abner Blossom despite the fact he had no appointment with the composer, and might be turned away.

"Do you happen to know if Mr. Blossom is entertaining tonight?" Val asked the receptionist in the front lobby.

"I believe he is free, Mr. Sturgis." The receptionist, who knew Val, was encouraging. "Why don't you go up. I'm sure he'll be happy to see you."

To Val's relief it was Abner himself who opened the door, and a pleased smile came over his face as he saw his pupil.

"You're just the one I am looking for," Abner began. "Come on in and sit over there near the piano. I want you to hear an aubade I have just written and which I aim to put into the opera I am writing. . . .

"Zeke," Abner called loudly, "bring Mr. Sturgis and me some refreshments."

Val sat back in a large green chair, and thanked Ezekiel effusively as the attendant brought him a large glass of French wine and a biscuit.

Abner had already seated himself at the piano when Zeke spoke in a somewhat scolding tone: "Let me adjust the piano stool, Mr. Blossom. It's at the wrong height."

"Ezekiel is as ever a perfectionist." Abner rose while his servant adjusted the seat.

Thanking Ezekiel and sipping a mouthful of wine, Abner then struck a few chords, and plunged into his new aubade.

The composition was so in harmony with Val's anguish of the moment that though he tried not to weep, a few tears spattered down his cheek.

At the composition's end, Val applauded vehemently.

"It's perfect, maestro," Val went on applauding fervently, and then took deep swallows of the wine.

Pleased by his pupil's praise of his composition, the composer swung round on his stool and stared at his pupil.

"What's wrong tonight, Val?" Abner inquired. "Something's worrying you I can see."

Val gave out a few evasive words.

"I know when something's wrong with a friend," Abner went on. "Do you think I can't smell trouble a mile away. And besides, it's not your habit to pay me a call at this time of the evening."

The composer folded his arms and waited for Val to unburden himself.

Val got it all out at once, and as he told of Luigi's leaving him to go to the dark-room at Cyril Vane's, he saw suddenly how ridiculous it must appear to someone as sophisticated and worldly as Abner Blossom.

"I suppose you'll blame me for having sent you there in the first place," Abner began. Then in a consoling manner: "But look at it this way. Cyril Vane, no matter what will happen, soon tires of everything and everybody. He has lived his whole life for pleasure and diversion. The only person he has not been able to banish is Olga Petrovna. Why he has lived with that harpy for over forty years, who knows. She may be the only element of reality in an otherwise drama of unending delight which is his life, pleasure, ceaseless satin-smooth pleasure!"

"You don't think then Luigi will go over to him?"

"What on earth do you mean by go over to him, pray tell," Abner sneered and tasted his wine suspiciously. He had discovered a tiny piece of cork on the rim of the glass. "Besides, my dear Val, you'll have some gorgeous photos of your Luigi for all time. For your own sake, don't be sad! I've never seen you so stricken. Be glad all the same you can feel this deeply for someone! Think what it will do for your music!"

Val was aware then of a certain lessening of his sorrow, but he knew the moment he left Abner's hotel, the pain would begin again until Luigi returned, if, he thought, he ever returns.

"Let's hear now one of the compositions you're at work on," Abner changed the subject, and ushered his disciple to the piano stool.

The visit to Abner Blossom had been a kind of benediction to Val Sturgis. He was calm and resigned as he left the Hotel Enrique. He felt he could face any contingency, and playing his new songs for Abner had made him realize again that his whole life after all was music. On reaching his apartment he fell into a deep sleep.

It must have been hours later that he was awakened by a

sound in the room. He saw Luigi seated under an old floor lamp. Val studied his friend. Luigi was completely absorbed in his study of the photographs. He would look at one for a while and then at another, and then begin again all over from the beginning to give each photo his fixed attention and scrutiny.

Looking up, Luigi said softly, "So you're awake at last."

He put the photographs away now.

"How did the evening go, Luigi," Val wondered, getting up now and throwing on his frayed dressing gown with the broken belt.

Val's eyes rested on the pile of photos.

"It was a long evening of waiting mostly. A couple of black opera singers were there, and they had center stage. I must have waited three hours as they strode over the red carpets and kept smelling the bouquets of roses Mr. Vane had given them. They were terribly fat, but they had piled themselves into corsets which kept giving out a smell of heliotrope. While I waited my turn, his assistant – "

"Harlan Yost," Val prompted when Luigi fumbled for the name.

"Harlan Yost," Luigi went on, and then stopped.

"May I look at these?" Val inquired.

Luigi suddenly took the photographs and held them against his chest.

"If they're something personal, Luigi – " Val recoiled now almost as if his friend had slapped him.

"I have been meaning to tell you, Val," Luigi began and then stopped.

Val seeing Luigi was in some fearful turmoil put his hand on Luigi's shoulder, but the younger man pulled away.

"I have a lot of explaining to do," Luigi tried again. "Oh well, go ahead and look at the photos," he finished and nearly threw the stack of pictures at Val.

The composer took the photos to his armchair and turned on the light and began looking through them.

"I can tell they're by Cyril Vane," Val began, and then as he looked up at Luigi he added, "Aren't these of the old-time movie star Francis Beauregard?"

"Old-time," Luigi said bitterly. "Well, yes," he admitted angrily. "I guess you're right."

"Did you ask for the photos? They must be very valuable. I assume Francis Beauregard is dead of course."

"He wasn't when I left him," Luigi replied.

Val put down the stack of photos.

"As I say I have been meaning to tell you," Luigi tried to begin, but then he saw the effect all of this was having on Val Sturgis.

"I have been living with this gentleman for some time. Before that I was several years in a monastery. . . ." Then sleepily like someone talking to himself: "Before that I lived in Sicily with my grandfather, and before that. . . ."

Val had barely heard anything after Luigi had told him he had been living with Francis X. Beauregard.

"He was certainly a very famous movie star," Val managed to sound slightly idiotic.

"It is all over," Luigi said.

"What is?" Val cried standing up.

"It was Harlan Yost I guess who gave the show away," Luigi also rose now. "He was trying to entertain me while I waited my turn to be photographed. Then I saw these photos. I blabbed I guess, and Harlan Yost told Cyril Vane I was a friend of Francis Beauregard's."

"And what did he think of that?" Val managed to ask.

"I told Mr. Vane everything I guess I have told you. He acted very odd about my disclosure."

"No wonder," Val said sarcastically.

"What do you mean by that," Luigi began to storm. "Are you judging me? Francis found me just the way you did. And I went home with him."

"And stayed," Val put in.

"Yes, stayed.

"Do you know something, Val. You act like God Almighty. I've never met anybody who judged everybody so strictly. So I lived with him. Maybe I loved him. I had seen his movies when I was only a boy in Sicily. Then to run into him like that, and be invited to his place in the wilds of Brooklyn somewhere. Yes, I stayed with him until I ran off carrying his busted umbrella in the rain. . . ."

Val lay down on the bed.

Luigi came over and lay down beside him.

"Cyril Vane was as dumbfounded at my having lived with Francis Beauregard as you are, Val. He too I guess thought Francis was dead. It changed everything between us. Or the old photographer was already exhausted by his session with the black sopranos, for all he did was photograph me with every stitch on while Harlan sort of bossed both of us around."

At the last, Luigi yawned violently. After all it was nearly four o'clock in the morning.

"'You'll have to come back again, Mr. Cervo,' Cyril Vane said as he ushered me out, 'when the hour is not so late and the studio is not quite so crowded as it was tonight. Meanwhile,' Mr. Vane told me, 'you may keep the photos of your friend, Mr. Beauregard. Put these photos in an envelope for Mr. Cervo, Harlan, if you please.'"

Cyril Vane and his assistant Harlan Yost were busy in the developing room a few days after Mr. Vane had photographed the black sopranos and Luigi Cervo.

Mr. Vane was in a jovial mood because for one thing Olga Petrovna had left for Atlantic City.

"Of course," Mr. Vane went on talking, "I never dream of yearning to know why Olga goes to a place which is in its way as tawdry as Coney Island. One would hardly believe, I always say to Olga, that a woman who claims to be a distant relative of the Romanoffs would be partial to Atlantic City when she has her choice of several European capitals.

"But then," the old photographer went on, "the black sopranos were asking me to reminisce about my days in the twenties."

"And the speakeasies! You were describing the speakeasies," Harlan Yost said and could see a strange look almost like that of pure joy as Cyril continued:

"There were I'm told twenty thousand."

Harlan grinned.

"Don't you know, Harlan, some authorities say there were even thirty thousand of them." Cyril laughed. He felt so comfortable with Harlan Yost. "And I daresay thirty thousand is more like the actual number."

"I hope you visited every single one," Harlan exploded in laughter.

The door opened and one of the early morning servants brought in an envelope marked

TO BE DELIVERED BY MESSENGER.

Harlan accepted the letter and handed it to Mr. Vane.

"See who it's from, Harlan," Mr. Vane suggested.

Harlan took a quick look. "No return address, sir."

"Well, why don't you open it."

Harlan produced a rather long communication on very thick vellum paper. He handed the letter to Mr. Vane.

"Perhaps you'd better read it. I've mislaid my glasses. But tell me – is there a signature?"

"It's from Mr. Francis X. Beauregard."

Mr. Vane stared at the letter in Harlan's hand. "I had no idea Mr. Beauregard was still living," he reflected.

"Go ahead, Harlan, better read it while I look over some of our photos here."

It was when he was reading the letter from Francis X. Beauregard that Harlan Yost became finally convinced of what he had only suspected earlier, that his employer was beginning to fail. Of course Mr. Vane had busied himself with developing the photos as Harlan read the letter, but that was not what had prevented him from listening to the words of Mr. Beauregard. Like Olga Petrovna the night of the opera, Harlan saw all too clearly Cyril Vane was as far from the present as if he were back in the days of the twenty thousand speakeasies.

Sensing all at once that his mind had wandered during the reading of the letter, Cyril inquired brightly:

"Can you summarize, briefly, the letter, dear boy, for these photos have absorbed all my attention."

Harlan nodded and rang for one of the servants. Then he began reading the letter again.

The servant brought in some morning coffee, and Harlan served Cyril a cup and waited until he had sipped some of it.

Harlan read on and on. Some of the peculiarity and the outrageousness of the letter was coming through.

"Oh, just summarize it, Harlan. It's written in the style of some sentimental novel of the 1910s."

Harlan needed all of the strong black coffee that the servant had brought. He drank an entire cup before going on with the letter.

Snatches of the letter as he read and repeated the phrases stuck in his mind. Cyril from time to time asked him to repeat them.

"I have it on good authority," the letter read, "that you have made the acquaintance of a young man who has been in my employ."

Looking up he saw Cyril holding up in admiration one of the finished photos of the young man in question, Luigi Cervo.

"This young man had no right to leave my employ," Harlan read on aloud in a hurried loud voice.

Cyril smiled.

"Would you please, dear Cyril, advise the young man that I am expecting his immediate return. No questions will be asked, no recriminations will be in order. I am desperately – "

"Desperately?" Cyril inquired.

"That is what the letter says," Harlan responded.

It was then too that Cyril Vane realized how deep in the letter Harlan Yost was, and he smiled appreciatively.

"Ah, Harlan," Cyril said gazing at the letter as if it were speaking all of this, "in my day I would have certainly written about a famous movie star begging for the return of a wild

Sicilian youth – if, that is, they would have dared publish such a story way back then . . . but I interrupted you. Go on with your reading."

"The needless suffering on my part certainly deserves his explaining why he left my home here, where he had every comfort and need satisfied. No sacrifice was too great, no – "

Harlan looked up to see Cyril's attention had wandered again. None the less he read on:

"Luigi Cervo is of course not a thief, not light-fingered, in fact he was before he came to me in a monastery, and. . . ."

Harlan waited to see if any of this was getting through to Cyril, whose face and eyes had the rapt expression they sometimes displayed when he listened to music.

"I will be ever grateful, ever in your debt, dear Cyril, if you can persuade Luigi to return to me. I am at my time of life, quite and solely dependent. . . ."

Harlan stopped reading to see if Cyril's attention was any longer on the letter.

"What should we reply to this letter?" Harlan wondered at last after waiting a lengthy time for Cyril to make some comment.

"Ah well," Cyril shrugged, and went back to looking at the photos carefully.

"Letter or no letter we must invite the young runaway back for another session, don't you think, Harlan?" the photographer finally spoke. "I have not seen a subject so right for my lens in many a day."

"But what should we reply to Mr. Beauregard?"

"Send him one or two of the photos. Not the best ones. The ones in this pile here."

Harlan stood gazing at his employer, a look of disappointment and grief on all his features.

"We can't very well send someone back to him," Cyril spoke now like his old self, "if that someone wanted to run away in the first place, can we?"

Estelle Sturgis, Val's grandmother, who had supported him at the Conservatoire in Cincinnati by telling fortunes, reading Tarot cards and by even more questionable practices, had often told her grandson that in cases of some serious illnesses, poison sometimes has to be prescribed to kill poison.

His grandmother's words were ever present now to Val as he lay seriously ill with a fever of over 101 degrees.

The doctor came and went, but Luigi Cervo never left his side.

Often Val would wake up in the middle of the night and find to his inexpressible comfort Luigi holding his hand looking down on him as benevolently as Estelle Sturgis had long ago.

Val had thought he had lost Luigi, but suddenly here he was never far from the sick bed. And though Val was certain Luigi did not love him in the overpowering way Val loved Luigi, the composer was nearly convinced Luigi cared for him perhaps more than anyone else had ever cared with the exception of Estelle Sturgis herself.

"You won't leave me, Luigi, will you?" Val had often cried out when he was delirious.

Perhaps then remembering his grandmother's remedy, that poison can kill poison, one evening when the patient was a little better and tasted a few mouthfuls of a strained beef and barley soup Luigi had prepared, the composer said in a steady if changed voice: "Maybe if you told me all about it, Luigi, I might understand it all and understand you better."

"You already understand all there is to me, Val."

"No, you don't understand. If you told me all about you before we met that night in the rain."

"But haven't I told you most of it. Told you all about the monastery and my granddad and me in Sicily."

"Told me about your love for Francis X. Beauregard," Val muttered.

Luigi frowned angrily and rose. Then perhaps remembering how serious Val's condition was, or perhaps not wanting to lose Val when he had found here the safest haven he had yet known, Luigi returned to the sick man, and stroked his head.

"If you want to know about me and Francis X., well, why not, Val. But when I tell it to you, you have to keep one thing in mind, that part of my life is all over. My life with you is the important thing now."

He bent down then and kissed Val on the forehead.

Then Luigi, sitting rather stiffly in the big armchair and looking a bit like a witness in a court of law, began.

Everybody or nearly everybody even then kindled to the name of Francis X. Beauregard. He had had a brief but dazzling career playing roles as diverse as Tarzan, and other gods of the jungle, a Martian Adonis, and several underground films which dealt with topics totally taboo in that era. Beauregard's age was not known, some sources saying he was eighty, others that he would never see sixty again, and still others claimed that he was still a rather young man owing to his having become a movie star at the age of nineteen.

Francis had a fair skin which had reminded Luigi Cervo of those bars of white chocolate one saw in candy factories in Sicily.

The way the screen idol found Luigi was different from the way he made contact with most of the young men who dwelt in his forty-room house in deepest Brooklyn. Beauregard had purposely chosen the most dangerous and neglected section of the old borough, near the Williamsburg bridge, and then filled the mansion with young men who waited on him hand and foot as if he were their supreme commander. He found most of his servants in pool parlors or dwelling in condemned vacant buildings, or sometimes even as dishwashers in well-established Italian restaurants. Francis Beauregard would write a note to one of the handsomer of the dishwashers with a hundred dollar bill enclosed with Francis' telephone number. Usually the receiver of the note responded the same day he opened the envelope, and moved in with his few belongings usually carried in a worn shopping bag. They never left, rumor said, once they arrived.

Many passed into middle or early old age in one of the upper chambers. Others however vanished almost the same day they arrived, finding the atmosphere and the tarnished grandeur too unfathomable to endure.

Like Val Sturgis, Francis Beauregard had espied Luigi cowering under a cigar store awning during a downpour. Francis had stopped his antique motor car and ordered Luigi in. Luigi had entered the car as calmly and obediently as he would have acquiesced to a command from his Abbot in the monastery.

The ninety-foot by forty-five-foot chamber Beauregard took him to that day was supplied with a monstrous chimney in which Chimney Swifts had built their nest. The delicate birds often entered the room and partook of crumbs and dainties Beauregard flung to them.

The two men that day sat and studied one another. Strangely enough they sat nearly twenty feet apart but both men had their seats close to the great chimney.

"I was attracted to you," Beauregard began, "because you look so like one of my Chimney Swifts. Chimney Swifts are my only friends, I often think." As he said this Beauregard made whistling sounds, and stared at the chimney. But there was no response at that moment from the swifts.

Beauregard rose now with a cold ceremonious manner and rang a small bell.

"While we are waiting for some refreshment, why don't you go into the bathroom on your left, take off your wet clothes, and you'll find clean dry things there with a choice of bathrobes."

Luigi found the bathroom almost as large as the sitting room where he had just been "interviewed," and he put on one of the countless dressing gowns and tied the belt rigorously tight. (Later Luigi was to learn that Beauregard had nearly two hundred dressing gowns, none of them it was said were cheaper than 500 dollars a garment, and all imported some even from a remote section of Russia, gowns claimed to have belonged to the Romanoffs.)

"You are a Chimney Swift," Beauregard repeated to the half-asleep pick-up.

"What did you say?" Luigi inquired in a lordly if not antagonistic tone. He had opened only his left eye as he spoke and stared.

As a matter of fact, Luigi could not remember having been picked up. He had taken a strong drug from a gentleman who had earlier struck up a conversation with him in a down-at-heel movie palace.

"Chimney Swift! Chimney Swift! You are that you know," Beauregard replied with a strange menacing expression. "Kindly drink the drink the servant has brought you. It will stop you shivering."

Luigi gazed indolently at the drink.

All at once Luigi who had now opened his right eye caught sight of a collection of merry-go-round horses in the dark recesses of the room. Their orbs shone like rows of jewels in a fashionable gem store. He rose, walked abruptly over to the silent horses, and then bending down kissed their manes assiduously.

He came back now and sat at the feet of his host. Beauregard touched carefully at his hair and scalp for he feared lice and scabies from street boys, but Luigi's hair was recently and thoroughly shampooed. Beauregard sighed contentedly.

Without any further preparation Luigi told him he had run away from a monastery and feared the Abbot might have sent out looking for him.

"Nobody will find you here," Beauregard said after digesting the information about his leaving the monastery. "My house, my home is full of young men who have run off from somewhere. And let me tell you, the police are friendly with me."

Luigi now appeared almost to be creeping to the feet of this new benefactor.

"Your hair looks like something afire. Do you know it crackles with electricity as I touch it. Your hair is softer than any woman's."

Luigi's eyes fell on a large goblet resting on a tiny tabouret near him. He picked up the goblet and attracted by its rich hue, he touched his tongue on the rim briefly, then made a wry face.

"Can I order something more to your taste," Beauregard brought out the words gruffly now as if speaking to an unknown party on the telephone. When there was no response from Luigi, the movie actor raising his voice said, "I'll choose for you then," and turning struck a small gong near the merry-go-round horses.

Two men in early middle age with tightly fastened dazzlingly white aprons appeared.

"Is there any more of that goat's milk and rum drink, do you suppose?" Beauregard asked. Both men nodded and went out.

"I used to drink goat's milk with my granddad," Luigi addressed the wall.

Beauregard nodded abruptly.

"In Sicily," Luigi finished.

"Let me tell you something," Beauregard rose and stretched his arms up and then behind his back and yawned. "You are a Chimney Swift. Never saw anything closer to it than you."

One of the attendants brought Luigi a cup the rim of which was tinged with cinnamon and nutmeg.

Tasting the drink, Luigi grimaced.

"Not to your taste, I gather," Beauregard commented.

Luigi then drank greedily, and wiped his mouth with his fingers.

"You'll find a napkin to your right, if you look," Beauregard informed him.

Rising with the traces of the milk still on his mouth and chin, Luigi strode over to where his host was watching him, and without more ado set himself down in Beauregard's lap and threw his arms sleepily about the actor.

Beauregard for the first time in many months, perhaps years, felt a fresh current of life kindling in him. He carefully touched the woman-soft hair from time to time, and then delicately opening Luigi's dressing gown a trifle saw what Val Sturgis would later observe, the young man's very black nipples.

But then the sound of snoring! Luigi had fallen fast asleep against the matinée idol's chest.

It was that moment, Beauregard would later tell some

friends who played cards with him late into the night, it was that action by the Chimney Swift which sealed Beauregard's fate.

"The Chimney Swift alighted on me," he would chronicle the happening, "went sound to sleep, and do you know, his musical snores put me to sleep also. I needed no sleeping powder that night. We slept in one another's arms until the hired help wakened us for morning coffee. . . ."

At first Francis X. Beauregard only whispered his discovery, which he also called his conversion. Then finally picking up a book with huge inky letters titled "Patriotic and Legal Holidays," he squeezed in among the designated feast days the scribbled words

My inert heart has come alive.

Then throwing down the book, and speaking aloud as if the cameraman were there before him, he got out:

My inert heart is beating.

What Francis Beauregard did not realize at once was the fact that Luigi Cervo had almost at the same moment he came in contact with the movie star fallen as much under the spell of the film actor as if walking through a city street or a desolate woodland he had come face to face with the Good Shepherd. For, as a small boy, he had gone to cheap matinées and seen Francis X. Beauregard playing jungle princes, bandit leaders, gigolos in evening clothes, spending money as if it were tinfoil, and wearing diamond stickpins, and always like a talisman exhibiting the deep dimple in his strong chin, which was in Sicily said to betoken superhuman virility. As a moon-struck boy he had dreamed of that dimple.

Francis Beauregard was unable to explain to himself, he who had countless young men at his beck and call, why this young Sicilian wearing cast-off clothing and with dirt under all of his nails except his two thumbs (which looked queerly as if a manicurist had begun on these nails), why such a young man had exerted so powerful and irresistible attraction on his dormant self.

Later he tried to explain to himself, unsuccessfully, that he saw in Luigi one of the shepherds in the *Eclogues* of Virgil. There were actually even a few briars in Luigi's hair as if he had been living in the grass alongside his goats. It was the Sicilian in him, Francis tried to explain, but then he knew it was something older and deeper and more fearful than Sicily. For as Luigi saw in Francis something entirely beyond the pageant of this world, so did Francis see, in the runaway from the monastery, something untamed and feral, undisciplined and unowned, waiting for whoever was daring enough and beyond the reach of the decorum of society, to take him for his own!

That first night, then, together, as will happen when a prisoner is brought back to his cell and finds another prisoner unexpectedly waiting, the two prisoners could only at first touch one another, fearing that the other would disappear, leaving behind nothing to prove that the newcomer had ever been present. And then gradually both prisoners, starved for human contact, would approach one another silently, touch gingerly and then with famished embrace begin to hold one another in desperate stricture.

But only Luigi slept that night, a hard snoring, almost strangling kind of sound issuing from his white teeth pressed against the astonishing blood color of his fleshy but on the whole thin lips.

All Francis Beauregard could do in his own half slumber was silently, softly, imperceptibly touch the visitor in his arms but always too lightly to awaken his prize.

Occasionally that night as later, Luigi would say something in an unknown language (later Francis would learn it was an almost illiterate Sicilian Luigi spoke).

When at last the attendants had brought them coffee and outside people could be heard stirring in the broad light of day, the two men rose separately, like actors after a long series of Shakespearean speeches, and took separate chairs where they continued staring at one another as new prisoners in the penitentiary who as cellmates gaze also at one another inexplicably when out of their cells they sit down in a common mess hall.

But as he rose now to call one of his servants, Francis X. Beauregard slipped all at once and fell at the feet of the newcomer, his mouth falling against the bare toes. He touched with his lips both feet.

"No, no," Luigi gave a kind of wail. "I can't endure for you to shame me – "

Looking up in anguish, Francis mumbled some words of wonder, even alarm. Luigi shook his head. He had been trained in poverty, need, blows, starvation fare, whippings, injuries dealt by hard fists, humiliation, ridicule, despisals, attempts on his life, repeated often, but had never known till then even the most intangible show of affection, certainly never love, and to have a show now of such extravagance by one who had been as ideal as the Good Shepherd was beyond Luigi's strength to endure. He fainted away.

It was Francis' greatest joy to carry the unconscious visitor to an oversize couch where the actor had spent so many gruelling hours waiting for old age and death. He laid the unconscious Luigi down on several pillows stuffed with dried flower petals, and then felt his pulse, listened to his heart beat, smiling. He remained kneeling nearby and gazed at the face of the one person who had used effortlessly every arrow in Cupid's bow to make him, in his late maturity, the total devotee, slave, prisoner of the dirt-encrusted, swarthy, yet flecked somehow with gold whoever-it-was who had come out of nowhere to claim him for his own.

There had been days in the monastery when, weary of praying on his bare knees in a cold cell and weakened by days of fasting, Luigi feared to open his eyes for he knew he would see something from the other kingdom. When at last sweating and trembling and dry-mouthed, he opened his eyes he saw the Divine Mother. She was weeping for him, she was also giving him permission to leave the monastery if he so wished. She looked at his emaciated arms and limbs, his chest revealing the bones like her own Son's on the Cross of Death.

Another time when coming home in the small town in

Sicily to meet his grandfather he had lifted up a branch from a half-fallen tree and looking him full in the face was the Savior himself. Luigi had fallen at the Shepherd's feet, had felt indeed the actual flesh of the leg and the cool fragrance of the blood-stained nails. He lay happy then for hours, thin strings of saliva falling to the dry earth.

Now living with Francis, he was not certain if he had not died and gone not to the paradise promised by his own faith but to some other heaven inhabited by other gods.

As to Francis X. Beauregard, his perplexity was if anything as keen and corrosive. He felt indeed that one of the Chimney Swifts had through his long years of purgatory been given human form to reward him for his torment. Or perhaps he too thought he had died at last and inhabited one of the Islands of the Blest.

To mitigate to some degree such intense unhoped for happiness on the part of both of the lovers, Francis now allowed occasional visits from silent-screen stars of the forgotten past.

Francis tried to explain to Luigi that he permitted Greta Garbo to visit him (though she was not always glad she had come) solely because she permitted him to touch the lips that had also he was sure pressed against the mouth of Jack Gilbert, Antonio Moreno, and Robert Taylor. Garbo permitted him in fact to linger with his mouth on hers as Francis fancied he was tasting some of the fragrance that had been bestowed on her by Jack Gilbert.

Francis even permitted a spare almost skeletal beauty whom he called Kate of the Silver Screen to pass hours with him. Lately she had always come accompanied by a young Briton, Algy Devall, who gazed in a kind of silent hysteria at Beauregard whom he had thought long dead.

Today after Kate and the young Briton had departed, Francis began pacing up and down the room; something about the visit of Kate had upset him. He paced more agitatedly, looking about distractedly nowhere in particular.

Luigi at that moment feared Francis had forgotten him, and that when the actor came out of his funk he would perhaps not remember who he was or what he was doing here in this building of so many rooms and hallways, servants and messengers which formed the actor's extravagant headquarters. But finally turning in his agitation to Luigi, Francis cried:

"To think she was once beautiful. For she was! Oh, why did she have to come and let me see her as she is now! Do you know what I thought of, Luigi? Are you listening to me? Do you know what she reminded me of, if it is not too unchivalrous to say. Have you ever travelled through the deserts of our own Southwest and seen the skeletons of young cattle bleaching in the pitiless sun? Oh well, I see you have not. I see too it was wrong of me to compare her vanished beauty with cattle skulls. Forget it. Let me suffer my own sorrow in my own way." And sitting down Francis Beauregard began weeping silently.

Luigi cautiously approached the chair Francis was seated in. Very often as now he was afraid his idol would look up and say "What are you doing here," or "Who are you." The drama would then be finished, and as in so many other houses where his hosts had said to him in the past: "There is the door! Depart!"

But his idol kept him to him, held him with those still strong arms and touched him with painful kisses.

"*Rondinella*, swallow," he imitated Luigi's own Sicilian. "*Rondinella*!" They stayed in a strange embrace for what to the servants seemed an endless time.

Finally one of the Jamaican youths whom Francis had also found on the street brought them out of their rapture by offering them a tray of food.

Francis stood up. "Ah, yes, the body clamors, urges, needles, nettles. . . ." He picked up a drumstick and to Luigi's astonishment ate it ravenously, then putting down the bone, gazing at it, cried: "Bones – our only immortality!"

Luigi, toward morning, while pressed close against Francis X. Beauregard, had a dream so troubling he awoke in a shivering sweat, shaking so violently that his lover had to go downstairs and bring up several blankets. It was only hours later that Luigi could remember part of the dream. Foolishly he told it to F.X. as he now sometimes called him.

"I dreamed I was carried away from the monastery by a

huge golden Griffin whose claws however did not wound me. He put me down in a palace of five hundred rooms. But I angered the Griffin by writing on a huge blackboard *The trouble with Paradise is it is Perfect. And Perfect is Dead.*"

Too late Luigi saw the effect of his dream. Francis drew away from him as if he had been touched by a sheet of ice.

Anyhow it was the day the Chinese doctors or herbalists or whatever profession they practiced arrived.

The two Chinese doctors looked as if they were identical twins.

Francis had told Luigi he might watch if he cared to, but he said this in a cold disdainful tone, then seeing the look of pain on Luigi's face, he relented and kissed him in a ceremonious fashion.

One of Francis' idiosyncracies was his collection of lavish bathrobes. He must have had a different bathrobe for each division of the day, indeed Luigi never saw him wear the same bathrobe twice.

"I will be in the room above," Francis told him, and left in the company of the Chinamen.

A new servant was serving Luigi his breakfast, but under the saucer of the king-size coffee cup Luigi's eye fell on a note in Francis' hand. It read: "I am the one who will always love you in any case."

Without finishing his breakfast Luigi hurried up the windingly steep stairs to the room above. The door did not give so he knocked.

One of the Chinese doctors unlocked and threw open the door, bowed, and ushered Luigi to a wooden chair. But Luigi was unable to suppress a cry as he looked toward the center of the room. There stood his idol without a stitch, spread-eagled against a huge wooden pale-yellow backdrop. At first he could only feel amazement that a man as old as Francis X. could look in the flower of his youth, and then, his eyes caught sight of a collection of needles sticking out all over the former actor's body. Luigi swallowed, began coughing, shook his head. Francis smiled weakly, encouragingly to him, while he looked as helpless and moribund as a Saint Sebastian.

A servant entered bearing the rest of Luigi's breakfast and poured hot coffee in a demitasse, which Luigi immediately drank off like a man who has suffered heatstroke and maddening thirst.

The needles had now been removed, and the Chinese doctors hastily began lighting small incense cones and placing these on different parts of the body of the actor who meanwhile never took his eyes off Luigi.

Luigi kept drinking swallow after swallow from the demitasse, always refilled by a servant's hand.

A kind of exhausted horror filled the young man finally when, the burning cones having been removed, he saw the Chinese doctors advance toward the pinioned actor with small whips. They beat Francis with rhythmic almost musical sounds. Upsetting his last demitasse, Luigi rushed from the room, and went back to where he had been sleeping with Francis. A paroxysm of icy nausea swept over him. He must have finally fallen asleep for, waking with a start, he judged by the light feebly entering through the giant shutters, day was passing into early twilight.

Francis appeared all at once in evening clothes, and with what Luigi disappointedly observed must have been a slight touching up of his lips with rouge of some sort.

Seeing the look of disapproval, Francis explained: "No, it is not lipstick, but salve. I always bite my lips I'm afraid when undergoing treatment. I'm sad it did not amuse you."

Luigi bowed his head, and Francis grasped his hand.

"How cold your fingers are."

Luigi buried his head in the actor's shirt front.

"So I have feet of clay," Francis said in a toneless voice. "And you have found that paradise is only perfect, not satisfying."

"It was only a dream," Luigi faltered.

"Only," the actor gave out a kind of snort. "No real dream is *only*."

And again to Luigi's bitter disappointment Francis burst into tears like a woman.

Luigi kept thinking of the sight he had glimpsed of the

actor's physique, like something an ancient Greek artist might have wished for as a model. But the cold again invaded his veins, and he shivered.

"I'm not going out after all," Francis exclaimed, and took off the jacket to his evening clothes. "No, no, I will stay here with you in our broken Paradise."

Time had stopped for Francis X. Beauregard, but time had not yet begun for Luigi Cervo.

After the first days and weeks of the intoxication of happiness Luigi felt a kind of languor, weakness, constant drowsiness. He began to fear that happiness itself was a kind of sleep, for here beyond his further imagination the idol of his boyhood had come into his life to claim him above every other human being. Yet everywhere in this splendid if tarnished mansion he shared with the star, only yesterday was enshrined, only yesterday remembered. There was no tomorrow here, hardly even really any present.

When Luigi had fled his Abbot and the monastery, though the pain was great, the feeling of betrayal intense, yet he had felt alive, and young. Even his pain was heartening and vital. Here where his every need was satisfied he felt the cool dank breath of the mausoleum. And gradually to his distress he found he could not really love Francis X. The very fact he looked so young, almost younger than himself, had a sort of death-like pervasiveness.

At first Francis X. did not perceive what was coming to pass. He was like Luigi so engulfed in an unexpected happiness, in an unbelievable return of love, that all else in his consciousness was blotted out.

But gradually, even after their most impassioned lovemaking, Francis saw all too plainly his young visitor's misery and malaise.

Sometimes Luigi would wake up from a heavy slumber and see Francis worriedly studying his features. Once he even caught him listening to his heartbeat.

Then one day when Luigi was leafing through a tome

devoted to the great silent screen stars Francis had known, staring at names and photographs of Barbara La Mar, Vilma Banky, Viola Dana, persons who obviously had been world-famous and who were today known to no one living except perhaps Francis, all at once the screen star removing the book from Luigi's grasp, said in a low but carrying voice: "You no longer love me."

In some panic he was unable to explain to himself, Luigi threw himself down at the actor's high shoes and held on to his ankles with such force Francis pushed him away.

"Please, please," came the smothered words from Luigi.

"I will love you though to the end of time," the actor spoke in a lifeless voice as he had sometimes done in his silent pictures for no one would hear in those days what expression he put into his voice, for only his image was transported to the millions who watched him.

"I will never leave you," Luigi's voice vibrated through the room.

"Get up, please, get up."

Luigi slowly rose as if the weight of all of Francis' own memories were upon him.

"I knew it would not endure," the actor went on. As he rose he dropped his book of photos and left the room.

Luigi felt the same way he had when one day in his cell in the monastery he could no longer pray because he no longer believed. Indeed he had never believed, he knew then. At the same time he felt that Jesus might appear to him.

Now a kind of Jesus *had* appeared, had gathered him against his beating heart, had given him a love he had never known mortal persons could experience, and yet he wanted to leave, not only wanted to but must leave. And he knew that by leaving he would be the destroyer of Francis's own life, certainly of any happiness the screen idol might ever hope for in the future. Luigi no longer believed in any case that he was even here.

He could not live in a timeless world, with a timeless lover even though in that timelessness he had experienced the greatest happiness he could know. Yet it was a happiness which outstripped his human and physical being. With Francis he had left the world and all that was him and gone into a deathless but deathly sphere.

He looked around the room in desperation. How could he leave all this. It would kill him. Yet if he did not leave he already was prisoner in death's kingdom, loved by death itself, caressed by a man who was more beautiful than any other man who had lived yet whose beauty itself was from some fearful, stagnant underground river. He thought of Orpheus and knew he must not look back now or his phantom lover would claim him forever and in his arms he would not so much die of happiness as he would vanish as himself under a love that would obliterate *everything* – wretched though that everything might be, it was himself, miserable tatterdemalion ignorant Luigi, yet in the end the only thing that was him, the only being he possessed, Luigi himself.

"If I could only die, Luigi, with my lips pressed against yours, how sweet death would be. Never leave me, if you don't do another thing in your life – stay here with me. Is it too much to ask?"

That was the last thing Francis had asked of him.

That night taking only a broken umbrella and the clothes he had on his back, Luigi Cervo left Francis and his kingdom behind him. He thought several times of looking back, but then a superstitious dread of doing such a thing prevented him.

A few hours later drenched to the skin, shivering, he had set eyes on Valentine Sturgis.

Luigi's long narrative of his running away from the monastery and running away from Francis X. Beauregard brought a chill to Val.

The change in the composer was communicated at once to Luigi who feared Val would turn him out.

"Have I spoiled everything," Luigi inquired, sitting down close to Val.

"I still love you if that's what you mean," Val responded.

Luigi nodded. But everything had changed, and they both knew it.

Val knew, like Francis Beauregard knew, that he would never love anyone as deeply as he loved the Sicilian, but he also knew that their love was already under some sentence of doom. It was with this knowledge that Val almost pushed Luigi into Cyril Vane's arms.

Cyril Vane had already telephoned Val Sturgis repeatedly, informing him of the letters he was receiving from Mr. Beauregard with regard to Luigi's having left the screen actor without reason or explanation.

A few days before Luigi's narrative of his life, Val would have forbidden Luigi to return to Cyril Vane's house, would have been outraged that the old photographer was planning more photographs of his lover. But having heard Luigi's narrative, Val had already agreed to relinquish his right over his lover, had already given up all claim to his love.

Val felt with calm terror a kind of death in his own veins. He had lost Luigi even more completely than had Francis Beauregard.

Cyril Vane greeted Luigi very much like a priest who is expecting a communicant for some special sacrament arranged long beforehand. Harlan Yost also welcomed him with a queer solemn ceremoniousness.

They saw him, he realized, as someone who had dwelt with the dead, who had now returned from the dead, and must if for no other reason be photographed as a testimonial.

Strong drinks were brought out, though Luigi barely tasted them and needed no stimulant to begin telling Cyril Vane even more about his life than he had told his lover Valentine.

Cyril Vane, who after all had been a brilliant novelist before he turned to photography, drank it all in, relishing every phrase, every scrap of the narrative which had broken Val Sturgis' heart.

As Luigi stripped off the last of any clothing he had on, Cyril Vane did not even need to tell this model where to stand or how to look, whether to smile or frown, grin or laugh, weep or sob. When Luigi took his position before the camera, every expression he assumed was the right one.

But there was one moment in the photographic session that

brought a deep silence from Cyril Vane, and his hand moved away from the camera.

It was when Luigi spoke perhaps to himself, certainly for himself under the blinding lights of the studio.

"Francis Beauregard always called me the Chimney Swift," Luigi offered this recollection. "In Sicilian, I told him, we say *rondinella*. After that he always repeated the word in Sicilian."

The photographer was thoroughly drained at hearing the story. Long after Luigi Cervo had left, Cyril sat on sipping Armagnac. The session had brought back with it his own remembrance of a brief but tempestuous evening with Francis Beauregard.

Harlan Yost was meanwhile observing his friend and employer with nervous anguish.

"I am afraid he will die," Cyril said at last, and gave Harlan a look of eloquence such as he had never seen on Cyril's face before. "I mean," Cyril explained smiling faintly at Harlan's sad expression, "I only mean, Harlan, I took a quick look at his right palm."

"And what did you see?" his attendant said morosely.

"Well, first of all, of course, he is a born runaway," Cyril replied looking out the window into the stretch of the park. "But I never saw such a life-line on any hand before, did you?"

Harlan who had not looked at Luigi's hand did not reply.

Cyril Vane like so many wealthy persons actually did reside somewhere, lived somewhere, was established in a fixed abode, looked forward to residing and living there indefinitely, felt indeed assured as well as comfortable, and therefore saw the world from a relaxed permanent vista looking down on the rest of humanity as a kind of Jupiter, who though interested in human activity and even concerned with some special individuals, took nothing too seriously and troubled himself only mildly with the sorrows and calamities of those he loved.

On the other hand as Luigi often told Val Sturgis from time to time, sometimes breaking off into Sicilian: "*We*, dear friend, unlike Cyril Vane, live like travellers who are sure of no abode for more than a night, ever wondering what tomorrow will bring and can count on only one thing: tomorrow will not bring comfort, security, peace, rest, or stability of any kind. I know what Jesus was talking about when He mentioned that foxes have holes and the birds nests while He had not a place to lay His head. That is the Jesus I worship and whom the Church never knew nor ever will know. The gatherer of young men who like Him had no dwelling or fixed abode, no place to lay their heads except in His Bosom. Oh how much I would have loved to have been His Disciple. I would never have left Him for in His presence I would have found a place to lay my head."

Val Sturgis tried not to fall into despair when he heard Luigi's strange soliloquy – which he longed nevertheless to put into musical form.

"But we have a place to lay our heads here, dear Luigi." Val tried to speak equably and encouragingly.

But he saw then what all who ever knew Luigi did see. Luigi would never have a fixed abode, he would belong nowhere, he would keep passing from one failed love to another because he had not lived in the same time of the Good Shepherd who like him and only like him had no place to lay his head.

Rushing then to Luigi's side, Val held him in his arms and smoothed his long tangled hair with its cowlick and the untrimmed eyebrows and black curling eyelashes. Val could hear his own heart thundering, each beat warning him he would not have Luigi for long. He did not need like Mr. Vane to look at his friend's outstretched palm to know he held in his arms one who was forever a runaway.

The way Olga Petrovna and especially Harlan Yost looked at Cyril Vane confirmed in his mind what Cyril Vane already knew. He had been passing for some time from green old age to white hoary old age. Not only Olga and Harlan looked at him in that special way, his young models also seemed to be saying goodbye to him while stretched undressed before his eye they fancied they heard a heavy gong sound for the cameraman.

"Youth," Cyril often remarked to Harlan, "youth does not appreciate the moment and that is because youth thinks it has no end to moments, or to time. They will never die. Now I. . . ." But here Cyril Vane paused. He often lost the train of his thought now. "It takes so long to do everything," he complained.

Everything became more precious, longer, slower, timeless. He felt the angel sometimes touch him ever so lightly as he came out of his slumber or fell into it. Even the ticking of one of his heirloom clocks sounded slower, as if it too hated to count the minutes and regretted there were so few of them left.

"While youth," Cyril went on explaining to Harlan Yost, "thinks they will never run out of time, and so they appreciate so little. I did too in my day. Think of them!" he almost shouted, "Val and then his latest lover Luigi who ran off from being a monk, and then, can you believe it, was lover of the silent screen star Francis X. who must be closer to my age. I wonder if Francis feels as I do or having deceived old age so long like, say, Hermes, perhaps time does not have the preciousness it holds for me."

What perhaps alerted Cyril Vane the most to his approaching end was Harlan's melancholy, his tenderness, the occasional moist eye, and the kinder way he touched the photographer.

Looking in the mirror too Cyril saw something in his own features which gave him pause. He was not able to quite describe what he saw and the photos Harlan shot of him did not tell the truth either.

"The camera," Cyril once told Harlan, "is or can be, like words, a liar."

Harlan shook his head but said nothing. Harlan believed to

the end Cyril Vane was one of the great photographers and that his art was beyond truth or lies.

Meanwhile Olga Petrovna became more frenzied, drank more, entertained more young men and fashionable women at her private dining room at Rumpelkammer's. She became loudly notorious, either much disliked or greatly sought after as a "character." The more expensive her gowns were nowadays the less distinguished she actually appeared. But she knew, if those who enjoyed her largesse did not, that she acted so extravagantly only because Cyril Vane would soon be leaving her.

Her life which since her silent screen days had been lived only for Cyril Vane stretched out now beneath her like a precipice. It was she indeed who touched earth the most palpably. Death was everywhere for her in those last days. His dusky beating wings and dank breath kept her in a constant state of fearful tremulous agitation. If every moment now to her husband was sweet and precious, comely and perfect, each moment to her was painful and unendurable as if it were she who, stretched out on her death-bed, drew every breath with anguish.

"What will I, what can I do," she often broke forth with this statement in the midst of her regal entertainments with the young men or fashionable dames who, nonplussed by her soliloquy, would bite their lips and look away from their hostess in pained embarrassment.

Olga Petrovna sent Cyril to famous specialists, she called on Chinese herbalists and brought back strange tinctures and secret potions, which Cyril immediately threw down the drain.

She waited endlessly as people in war await the final bombardment or as early Christians expected the end of the world and time. As each minute and hour to Cyril was happiness, each moment of time to her was unending suffering. She felt like Atlas bearing the entire weight of the world's sorrow and with apprehension of yet greater sorrow to come.

The buzzer to his apartment rang frantically. At first Val Sturgis thought he would ignore it, but then, his inspiration having failed him for the day, and no notes forthcoming from his muse, he pressed the button to admit whoever it was arriving.

He could not disguise his surprise and also his uneasiness when Harlan Yost entered. Bad news was written all over his face.

"But I'm interrupting your work," Harlan apologized.

"As a matter of fact, Harlan, I was about to give up on what I'm composing, and go for a stroll along the docks."

Harlan nodded gloomily, wrapped in his own thoughts.

"Is something wrong?" Val wondered sympathetically.

"Something? Everything."

"Is it Cyril?"

"Isn't everything Cyril Vane where I'm concerned. Yes, it is, but mostly it's me. After I've spent my life waiting on him hand and foot, and now. . . ."

Val nodded and smiled encouragement.

"He's failing fast, Val. And he drinks so much. Then there is the Lioness of course, who's always been my cross. Olga Petrovna. She kills me with her scorn and contempt. She's off now again in Atlantic City, gambling I suppose or drinking or buying trinkets that would keep you and me in clothes and grub for several years.

"But I didn't come here, Val, to cry on your shoulder. Look here, will you?"

Harlan brought out a thick package tied with heavy cord.

"Go on, please, open it. It'll brighten both our days."

Harlan sat down while Val fumbling with nervousness began to open the package over which the name and address of Cyril Vane blazoned in imperial large letters.

Inside the package was photo after photo of Luigi.

Val looked at each photo with rapt attention, and then began going over the same photos again and again. Lost in admiration, he had forgotten Harlan Yost was even in the same room with him.

Val held one photo now close to his face, then coming out of his reverie, he said brokenly, "Thank you, Harlan. You will never know what these photos mean to me."

"Do I smell fresh brewed coffee, Val?" Harlan wondered, looking toward the kitchen stove.

Val got up at once, grinning, and poured his visitor a king-sized cup. Then he returned to the pile of photos and began touching them admiringly all over again.

"I can go on living now I have these," Val spoke more to himself than to his visitor. "I will write Mr. Vane my thanks and gratitude."

As the two men drank their coffee, which Val occasionally replenished from the glass pot on the stove, something in Harlan's manner drew Val's full attention to the secretary.

"You were telling me how worried you are about Mr. Vane," Val began. "Then the photos swept my mind off everything else."

Harlan nodded. "Whatever anyone may say about Cyril, we all have to admit he is a great photographer."

Val nodded, and his eye fell on the stack of photos of Luigi Cervo.

"Mr. Francis Beauregard keeps calling us to find out where Luigi is," Harlan went on.

"Why don't you tell him?" Val said, an angry bitterness coming into his voice. He stared again at the sheaf of photos.

"I think he has already found out," Harlan said.

Val bit his lip.

"I always have felt I could confide in you, Val," Harlan's tone changed so markedly that Val felt some stranger was speaking to him.

"I'm approaching the greatest crisis of my own life," Harlan went on. "I realize now that I have no one, or will have no one soon. I know Cyril will soon be leaving us. I'm thirty-eight, old for New York City, and all at once I wonder what I've been doing for twenty years in the employ of so resplendent, and larger-than-life a person as Cyril Vane. I've tried to give him gold, and yet I see now all he admires is tinsel if it's got style. And he's never cared as deeply for me as I have for him. But I love him, and can't change that for all his faults and short-comings. The only thing Cyril loves is gaiety and change of scene, sparkle and new faces; no wonder he is always speaking of the twenty thousand speakeasies!"

Val became so absorbed in what Harlan was saying he almost forgot his own misery over Luigi.

"I can't blame Olga Petrovna for being a harpy and a raving maenad. She gave up her career as a silent screen actress to be a fifth wheel on his never-never-land express. He needed a brakeman and a blind, and he has kept her. She is his flaming torch at the entrance of his city of the plains, so that the square world won't know he lives in ancient Pompeii. Besides where could Olga go now if he no longer wanted her to hold the torch. Back to the silent screen?"

Here Harlan broke into a paroxysm of coughing, and then drank off the rest of his coffee.

Harlan talked on and on, and Val made another pot of coffee. Before they knew it several hours had elapsed. Occasionally, even as Harlan spoke of his long years with Cyril Vane, Val would pick up one of the photos the photographer had made of Luigi.

"Thank you for letting me run on like this," Harlan said at last. "I knew the minute I saw you that evening of your first visit to the studio, you had a heart. Do you have any inkling who most of the people are who come to be photographed? Of course you can't! You're so much younger than me. And then," he too stared at the photos, "you have Luigi. Lucky lucky both of you."

"I'm afraid nobody has Luigi," Val said.

"Why do you say that?" Harlan wondered.

"Even when we seem to love one another so perfectly," Val spoke in an almost inaudible voice, "I can hear his heart racing and beating to be free, to resume his running and his fleeing. As he once said of himself, he's on a racetrack going nowhere at top speed."

Val smothered a shower of tears now with a blue working-man's handkerchief.

"Let them fall," Harlan spoke of the tears. "I admire

anyone who can cry. I was always punished by my Dad if I bawled, and see where it has landed me. As an amanuensis to an old hedonist who wouldn't miss me more than a minute if someone younger and prettier took my place. So, cry, weep, Val, if it soothes you. It soothes me to see you because I don't know how to let my tears fall."

"Those last days!" Those were the words Harlan Yost repeated so often. And even Val Sturgis, despite his belonging to such a different age, began to understand at least partially after his long conference with Harlan Yost that the end of something even larger than the life of Cyril Vane was approaching. The world was about to enter into a plainer, drearier, more tasteless, common and mean-spirited age.

As if she could not bear to see the end itself, Olga Petrovna chose to be always absent. She had intended as usual to stay in some twelve-room suite in a New Jersey resort hotel, a hotel which was also approaching its demise, but at the last moment she went on a Caribbean cruise with her old friend and arch-rival the Baroness Kerenyi.

If Cyril Vane had kicked up his heels in times past when his wife disappeared on another of her jaunts, suddenly Cyril as if he saw at last what others had foreseen for some time, announced calmly to Harlan: "The sky is the limit now, my dear friend. I must not be gainsaid, vetoed, or lectured or impeded. If you cannot go along with my plans, you may take Olga's lead, and go on vacation also!"

"Why on earth would you think I would interfere with whatever you are planning, Cyril?"

"I have always felt you were at heart a puritan like her," Cyril was abrasive.

Harlan looked away and then began to study the enormous guest list.

It began then. Hundreds of telephone calls first, then tele-grams, followed by flowers sent by messengers with regal com-mands to attend enclosed.

They came then by the carload, Harlan would remember. Hardly a white face amongst them. The doormen and the eleva-tor operators or in Cyril's phraseology, "the footmen," had been given perquisites of such liberality that not one of them dared raise the least hint of criticism or disapproval at the number and the character of the assembling guests.

It was so much more thorough-going, elaborate and ele-gant than an orgy. It was itself an opera of some kind, Harlan would later reminisce to friends.

Since Cyril Vane had loved both men and women indiscri-minately, as one old friend put it, his guest list for the blow-out comprised a liberal sprinkling of both sexes, paramount among whom was the noted mime Elijah Thrush who called Cyril's friends in his own *fin de siècle* phrases, the indeterminate sex.

The greatest hotel kitchens and the caterers who usually favored only royalty or the diplomatic corps or the presidential party, were busy night and day. The liquor emporia had not known such business since they operated for the better speakeasies when, as Cyril never tired of repeating in those golden days of cheer and glory, there were speakeasies on every corner.

"I have never gotten over my grief that that decade came to a sandpaper-dry close." Cyril was to repeat this statement end-lessly.

It was fitting that the mention of speakeasies was made again, for what occurred at Cyril's residence recalled the definite air of the illegal, the surreptitious, the crafty, even more than a hint of the criminal. Negroes had always of course been Cyril's enjoyment for the forbidden. But he had never been able to give his all to them so fully before. The chandeliers in his collection of suites first tinkled, then gave out octaves of chimes, and then finally threatened to come loose from the ornate gold-flecked ceilings and crash on the heads of the dancers, singers and trombonists whose notes and rhythms could be heard for blocks away.

"How many guests were there?" young men later would inquire tirelessly of Harlan Yost. "And did he photograph all of them?"

Harlan had to think.

"They came and went, you see. Some stayed the night sleeping on carpets as thick and comfortable as the finest mattresses. And when one guest left, two or three took his place."

In the end, as Harlan remembered, everybody was naked except one tremendously fat black woman, a diva from Paris and Martinique, who kept on her whale-bone corset but was otherwise bare.

"There was more kissing and nestling than actual intercourse," Harlan was to have testified later on. "But of course, with liquor flowing like a broken water main, there had to be the other, especially in the spacious comfort of Olga Petrovna's private suite."

Cyril himself had never been more grand, more beneficent and more than liberal. He looked like the Father of the Gods, having come down for the last time from Olympus. He seemed to be crying "Rejoice, be happy. All that matters is joy, unending joy. The rest is rubble. Joy! Joy!" And he would throw himself into the arms of some brawny boxer, or a new countertenor, or Harlem poet.

Ethel Waters, known then as Sweet Mama String Bean, the greatest blues singer of her day, entered all at once unannounced, and walking directly over to her host, clasped Cyril in her mammoth embrace. She shook her head in disbelief at the spectacle which surrounded her.

It was unending, indeed immortal like Cyril Vane himself, Harlan thought. Yes, he felt, it would go on forever, time itself being perhaps brought to conclusion.

There was one discordant note in the overpowering splendor, and Cyril at that moment made the only *faux pas* Harlan could ever remember.

All at once, unannounced, Francis X. Beauregard himself made his entrance. He was wearing evening clothes of vintage

1902, with an opera cloak lined with silk, and ruby buttons.

Cyril stared at the approaching film actor, and then having cautiously kissed Francis wetly on the lips and placed his photographer's hand on a sensitive place of the actor, cried: "Oh, tell me. You are not crossed over after all!"

Francis X. bridled, pulled his opera cloak about him securely, and attempted to reply, but instead bowed low, as if wondering if one of his many rings had come loose and fallen to the carpet.

Ages later Harlan did think Francis X. had said something like: "I was only waiting to cross with you, dreamboat."

Whatever Francis' remark was it brought a sudden change of expression to Cyril Vane's mobile features as if a cold wind had blown from the massive windows facing the park.

Then giggling at the screen star's witticism, and holding Francis to him as he had so many years past, he kissed the screen actor in his carnival fashion of that evening, and ordered more bottles of champagne to be uncorked. "To the most pulchritudinous screen star ever!" Cyril raised his glass but suddenly reeling a bit, fell again into the arms of one of the boxing stars of the period.

The free-for-all lasted a good week, Harlan later recalled describing the tempestuous carrying-ons to his small circle of friends. He especially loved to talk everything over with that attentive ear Abner Blossom and his pupil-disciple Val Sturgis.

But he even discussed it both while it was going on, and after it had ended with his own master Cyril Vane. "How long have we been at it?" Cyril would inquire at the height of the "circus." "We must not be having a blowout if Olga Petrovna is returning."

"Listen, Cyril," Harlan Yost began a day or two before the orgies came to an end.

"What is it, sweetheart?" Cyril wondered. Harlan looked at him with such worry that Cyril repeated the question.

"Nothing, nothing."

"Tell me what nothing is then."

"I have loved all of this, Cyril."

"I know you have."

"I have loved you too."

Cyril blinked and smiled. "But what is it, your nothing?"

"I've always hated the ballet, the classical ballet. I agree with Isadora Duncan about it."

"Oh why mention her now," Cyril scoffed.

"I wish to Christ I could have seen her. Lucky you, Cyril."

"Well I guess she was everything they say."

From inside they could hear someone playing the soprano sax, and another genius hard and loud at the 88.

"You never were nice when I photographed the prima ballerinas," Cyril reminded him.

"True, true. Could I help it?"

"I don't think from where I sit at present anybody can help anything. We come into the world pretty much the way we'll be throughout. If God had wanted us different wouldn't He have created us different? I don't know."

"But after those prima ballerinas I've had to watch you over the years documenting with your lens their skeleton frames with no breasts and thighs like after the meat is off the wishbone . . ."

"Oh, behave."

"No, no, let me. It's so late, let me. Then when you began with the blacks, and were the first not only to photograph them, but to do so with them wearing not a speck of clothing anywhere . . ."

Cyril's head fell over.

"Are you dozing, Cyril?" Harlan tried to keep the worry out of his voice.

"You sound like Olga Petrovna at the opera," Cyril opened his eyes. "Go on with your speech for pity's sake."

"I realized I hated the ballet and the prima ballerinas and even the young Hercules that lifted their aging bodies up over his head, such a cruddy cliché in art. How can anybody go on looking at that museum kind of art."

"So you were happy then with me because of my blacks."

"Because of you seeing them the way you saw them."

"They have moved me pretty deep, but I did admire the ballet people."

"You are a snob I suppose."

"And you're not?" Cyril said.

"I don't know what I am."

"Yes you do, Harlan."

Harlan watched him then hardly daring to draw breath. Something final was coming he knew.

"Why are *you* so crazy also about colored people, do you know?" Cyril spoke almost wide awake all at once, and motioned for Harlan to pour him another drink of bourbon, crushed ice, and a touch of rum.

"My great-great-granddaddy was they say an Indian."

"So you once said, but I knew it before you spoke to me that day you first came to me."

"It's so plain then?"

"Not to most people."

Cyril grinned. "Your cheekbones give you away."

Harlan wiped away a slight dribble of liquor from Cyril's pale lips with a Portuguese linen handkerchief.

"You know even royalty only goes back six hundred or seven hundred years, and then what were they before that time? We haven't the faintest notion of where any of us actually came from."

"You've been reading books again, I see," Cyril spoke sleepily.

"Shall I make you some coffee now."

"What for?"

"Don't you hear the sparrows and the mourning doves outside. We've sat through another night of it."

They listened then for a while to the doors closing and the elevator running.

"Make yourself some coffee and maybe I will join you. Meanwhile pour me another drink. Why you don't see anything in the ballet though is a bit puzzling because you know so much about everything."

"Taste is taste."

Cyril grunted.

When Harlan got into the kitchen Mrs. Purefoy had already arrived quieter than any thief in the night and was beginning to tidy up and she had the coffee already perking on the stove.

But perhaps because of her presence Harlan burst into sobs.

"Why Mr. Yost, sir," Mrs. Purefoy was taken aback by the force of his sorrow. "What on earth?"

Harlan did a thing then that pleased her and made him even happier, he leant down and wiped his tears on her big pink apron.

"Mr. Vane is not looking well, Mrs. Purefoy, don't you think?"

She dried her own hands now on the apron.

She nodded solemnly and served him a cup of coffee.

Harlan took it and walked carefully back to where Cyril was still sitting.

"Maybe when you're old you'll be more open-minded about everything," Cyril Vane said and Harlan knew then that he had deeply offended him by not liking the classical ballet and admiring too much Isadora instead.

Harlan Yost spent that night under Cyril Vane's roof. He seldom did this, certainly never when Olga was present. But Cyril had asked him to do so, silently, eloquently, a request not to be gainsaid or denied.

Harlan slept hardly a wink. In the early morning he could hear a work-crew cleaning up, moving furniture, washing windows, swearing occasionally, whistling, cursing.

He went to Cyril's bedroom but Cyril was not there. He wandered off into the vast reception room. In a plush armchair recently purchased by Olga Petrovna especially for Cyril the photographer was seated, half asleep, holding a telegram in his left hand, the one with the tarnished wedding ring. He held the telegram up when Harlan bent over him.

Harlan read it from Cyril's outstretched hand.

RETURNING THIS EVENING. DEVOTEDLY, OLGA.

Suddenly Cyril fell back against the chair, and the telegram slipped down to the floor. His mouth came open and his eyes focused helplessly on Harlan.

Hardly waiting to tell him what he was about to do, Harlan rushed to the phone in the hall and telephoned Dr. Graustark. One of the day-servants helped Harlan carry Cyril to his bedroom. He could not speak but kept signaling to Harlan with his child-like wide-open brown eyes, as clear and penetrating as ever, omniscient to the end.

Cyril patiently held Harlan's right hand in his as though Harlan were the one who was so ill. Then all at once the hand gripped him painfully, then relaxed, and fell to the sick man's side. A gasp came from his long-time companion and secretary.

It seemed a long time before the appearance of Dr. Graustark, an elderly bowed man who looked out at everybody and everything from thick white eyebrows with a kind of glint in one eye. He hardly needed to look twice at Cyril Vane, but he took the motionless hand in his, opened the closed eyelids, closed them again.

"You say Mrs. Vane is due here this evening?" the doctor addressed Harlan.

For a moment Harlan did not register who Mrs. Vane was. He had never heard her called so, she had never called herself so.

"Ah, yes," Harlan came out of his reverie at a look of impatience from the doctor.

"Will you be able to stay until the coroner comes and removes the body?"

Harlan nodded, trying to keep his eyes from looking at his dead friend and mentor.

The doctor gave him a final look of wonder and probably disapproval and said, "Goodbye then." Then before leaving the room he said, "It's fortunate you were able to be here."

"I don't know how he kept going this long with a heart in the condition his was in."

Harlan nodded slowly like a deaf person who only guesses what someone has said. The doctor's face relaxed a bit, then quickly assumed its cold professional lines. The doctor paused however before exiting, and going up to Harlan grasped his hand briefly and then went out.

The light had become dim in the room but Harlan sat on without lights. When it was pitch dark, Mrs. Purefoy tiptoed in, and lit a small lamp at the far end of the bedroom. "Won't you come into the dining room and have something, Harlan," she said. "'Twill do you good." She avoided looking at the dead man who was stretched out, with two blankets covering him. Harlan shook his head.

When it was so dark in the room that even the small lamp hardly illuminated anything, he heard those energetic angry footfalls, and looked up to see Olga Petrovna.

She ignored him.

She went up to the bed where Cyril lay. The star of *A Tale of San Francisco*, *The Return of Irma Green*, and other box office successes of 1914 and 1915 sat gracefully and lightly like a dandelion that has blown to seed, Harlan thought.

She began to rock herself back and forth.

"Yes, yes," she muttered. "Oh of course they had to let me know. And of course they had given me warning." She took out a pill case and slipped a purple pastille in her mouth.

"Water?" she finally spoke to Harlan, but Mrs. Purefoy entered just then and handed her a tumbler.

"Thank you, Della, thank you."

She rocked back and forth in the chair avoiding looking at the dead man.

"Borrowed time," she said to Della Purefoy. "That's where we are all now, dear. On borrowed time."

Harlan Yost took more special pains with his grooming the morning of the funeral than he usually did. He had always been well-groomed, none the less, since he had worked as Cyril

Vane's secretary and assistant. Cyril had sometimes joked about his impeccable appearance. "Not a hair out of place," the photographer had smiled.

But today while shaving Harlan looked up quickly in the glass because he had almost cut himself, and then for a moment thought he was gazing at a total stranger. His jaw fell, the hand with the straight razor (he prided himself on using one) fell to his side. "I recognized myself," he later was to speak to Val Sturgis. "I saw who I was. My long masquerade as an old man's underpaid factotum was ended. And who was I looking at. An almost full-blooded Ojibway Indian. Cyril loved niggers, why didn't he see an Indian was pretty damned far-off geography for him too."

It took him some time then to get himself together. He had met himself or, in other worn-out expressions which came to his mind, the scales had fallen from his eyes on the road to Damascus, and so forth.

The funeral was for high noon. The casket was closed and sealed. Harlan got there at eleven o'clock. There were not many flowers, he was relieved to see. He loathed flowers, even one solitary rose reminded him of the grave.

Olga Petrovna suddenly appeared in of all things a pale pink gown with a nondescript unflattering corsage. She gave him the same kind of look with which she read the entirely memorized menu at Rumpelkammer's, nodded and vanished. Later Mrs. Purefoy told him Madame Vane would be unable probably to attend the funeral service.

They came by the carload except for the speaker who was to pronounce Mr. Vane's eulogy. Olga had seen to that. There were to have been three speakers, Harlan noted, two from some high falutin' Transcendental Higher Culture Society, one from the Terpsichore Society, but only one showed up – Lionel Kremtorte.

Harlan had stationed himself at the main entrance to the seventy-foot-long drawing room.

Cyril Vane's funeral in the end made almost more noise than his accomplishments as a recherché novelist and photographer. The press reporters and the press photographers came from as far off as Honolulu, and especially from San Francisco.

The crowned heads of black culture were there barring none. All the great boxers (white too), all the most famous blues singers, opera singers, tap dancers, body-builders, vibraphone players, and a score of saxophonists and trumpeters.

The blacks outdid every one of the few white persons present in their attire, style, composure, grandeur. It made Harlan almost want to tell each one who entered and shook his hand that he was after all not to be overlooked as an Ojibway. He felt as redskinned then as everyone else was black.

Finally the notes from a small electric organ brought expressly for the service began their blurred, honied harmonies. A few sniffles were heard. The latecomers gazed quickly at the sealed coffin, and away, embraced Harlan as if he were part of the family, looked in vain for Olga, but dared not ask where she was.

As the notes of music were dying away, a door slammed somewhere and Olga Petrovna, wearing now a velveteen long black gown with diamond necklace and one diamond earring made her entrance, Olympian if stagey. A dead silence greeted her.

"One would think, would one not," she began, staring with rapt hatred at Harlan, "One would think would one not," she went on turning abruptly to the assembled mourners, "that *you*, sir" (brandishing her braceleted arms at Harlan,) "would believe that *you*, standing before us all like Mr. All-Important, were the bereaved widow, and not I."

She turned away from Harlan now to address the mourners, all of whom hearing her tirade had lowered their heads almost as far down as heads can be lowered so that they resembled persons expecting the guillotine.

"My darlings," Olga Petrovna began, changing from the tigerish inflection levelled at Harlan to a tearful but ominous tone that was even more unnerving. "I beg of you, my dearest friends, and beloved admirers of Cyril Vane, to excuse me, and pray pardon me if I do not sit amongst you in your grief. I am ill, my darlings, ill!" She burst into a few sobs. Those who had not been old enough to have seen her silent movie triumphs could not compare this Olga Petrovna with that far-off silver screen star. "I love all of you!" she cried stepping into the main part of the room. "Not one of you is anything but beloved!" She blew frantic kisses, then swept out of the large room but before exiting she delivered a look of such levelled hate and venom at Harlan that he closed his eyes and bowed low. Then he advanced into the room of mourners and sat down.

A eulogy was meanwhile in progress. The speaker, a gentleman from the Transcendental Higher Thought Institute who had been personally invited by Olga Petrovna, was reading laboriously from some notes. But instead of the usual kind of praise bestowed on one who has departed this life, Lionel Kremtorte launched into a thinly veiled criticism of Cyril Vane, pointing out the dead man's many failures to involve himself in the great social needs of the day, and instead, the speaker averred, Mr. Vane had made pleasure and joy the sole illuminating beacon of his long and self-indulgent life.

"He was, ladies and gentlemen, the leading hedonist of his day!" Mr. Kremtorte raised his voice against a low threatening murmur of disapproval coming from the mourners.

Unable to stand such an attack on his idol any longer, Harlan Yost made what was perhaps the supreme act of his sojourn in Manhattan. He rose with what he later thought must have appeared nearly as dramatic an interruption of the funeral as Olga Petrovna's earlier foray into the assembly of the grief-stricken.

"Not one word more, not a syl-la-ble or breath more!"

And seizing Mr. Kremtorte by the collar, Harlan Yost pulled the speaker away from the podium and forcibly pushed him toward one of the exits to the slow murmurs of approval and a few measured handclappings.

At that moment the most famous black Gospel choir in the nation raised its strong and reverberating lungs. They sang and sang, louder ever louder drowning, extinguishing to oblivion the jarring words of Lionel Kremtorte forever.

Then just as if in one of the black musicals of a bygone age all the mourners rose as one and began clapping and singing in perfect unison. Their voices shook the room to the extent that the great chandeliers, and the building itself vibrated, swayed, even threatened to come down.

But the voices of the Gospel choir did not quite drown out the sudden if not unexpected outcry of a faded but still powerful contralto, cracked but soaring somehow above the hundreds of black gospel throats.

"Darlings all, dearest beloved, I had to come out again. You are all dearer to me than life! Don't deny me, my precious ones. Let my love enfold you!"

As she spoke these words, Olga Petrovna stretched out her arms as if indeed she were gathering disciples to her shrunken sequined breasts.

"How my heart bleeds for all of you," she lowered her voice, and then began looking about for the eulogist, Mr. Lionel Kremtorte.

Harlan Yost now stepped forward, determined to banish Olga Petrovna as he had Lionel Kremtorte.

"Don't touch me, you delegate of the spires of Sodom!" she cried addressing Harlan. "Here is the man," she appealed to the mourners, "here he is, the one who stole the love and protective closeness of my late husband from me. Look at him, ladies and gentlemen. There he stands, he who usurped my place in my broken marriage, who led my beloved spouse to secret infamy and dissolute hidden pleasure!"

She struck Harlan Yost then full in the face, and not content with this blow she spat full in his face.

One of the hired mourners now came forward and tried to calm the widow, but she broke away from him, and turning to the assembled throng who had been gradually moving as far away from her as possible, she burst forth again: "I bless all of you, and beg you to remember that my love for you will continue, my doors will be opened to all of you just as his were. My love shall go with you for evermore!"

Both the gospel choir and the organ now drowned out every other sound.

Olga Petrovna was finally led to her own chambers by a trio of paid mourners and Harlan Yost, looking more regal and self-possessed than he had during his years with Cyril Vane, began assisting Mrs. Purefoy in handing out the libations and the cakes baked just that morning for the funeral guests.

Two famous heavy-weight boxers of the recent past, one white, the other black, now took Harlan's hand in theirs, and offered him heartfelt words of consolation.

But in the midst of all these expressions of sympathy, Harlan heard a high-pitched voice and taking a good look he saw approaching him Abner Blossom and his pupil Valentine Sturgis.

"Why, where on earth were you two gentlemen seated?" Harlan for the first time during the service began to sound like himself. "I can't tell you how relieved I am to see both of you here."

"We came sneaking in," Abner began in his booming manner, "just as Madame Petrovna was giving her performance from, I take it, a scene from *Medea*."

Val Sturgis put his arm around Harlan and hugged him lengthily.

"Please stay, gentlemen," Harlan urged the two composers in a kind of desperate entreaty. "We are having a special repast which was prepared especially for you. . . ."

Outside of applause and praise there was perhaps only one other thing Abner Blossom could never resist, dining in style, even when the occasion was such a sad one as the present.

However, Mr. Blossom hesitated briefly before accepting Harlan's invitation. "Will Madame be joining us, Harlan?" he inquired.

"No, no," Harlan was firm. "I presume from the manner of the doctor who just left she will be sleeping." Harlan hesitated. "I suspect he gave her her usual hypodermic," he added.

"Pity," Abner's voice boomed on. "She might have entertained us as we feasted."

The last of the black mourners had departed and a peculiar, heavy quiet descended.

Harlan ushered Abner Blossom and his pupil Valentine toward a small dining room which was situated as far from Olga Petrovna's suite as possible.

As they were seated sipping a rum concoction invented by

Cyril Vane for special occasions Abner, speaking as if he were at home in his own rooms at the Hotel Enrique, began: "They are able to predict the weather fairly accurately these days. They can tell us when the sun will shine, how many knots the wind will blow, and how high the thermometer will rise or fall, but no one can tell when one of us is to die, even when that someone is at death's door. I suppose we should all congratulate ourselves on medical science's failure to know. It would make everything quite jumpy, would it not if we knew when each of us was to join the choir invisible."

Harlan Yost began to feel a little more like himself, and Abner helped this feeling by occasionally pressing his hand and smiling.

Val Sturgis drank off his rum special, and acknowledged he would not mind another. An extremely tall black man wearing a pale lemon turban attended them now. The several gold rings on each of his hands attracted the eyes of Abner.

"Let us drink to our dear departed comrade," Abner rose proposing the toast after he had given the waiter a long thoughtful look. "We will miss him," he kept his eyes on the server, "and many will mourn him for some years to come."

The server bowed his head and said softly, "Amen."

The friends all drank now with solemn concentration.

"Why didn't Luigi come?" Harlan said more to make conversation than to discover where Luigi was.

Val hesitated lengthily. "Oh I didn't think it was the place for him," he explained at last.

"But I personally asked him," Harlan spoke rather airily.

A new waiter now brought in French toast, omelettes, slivers of pink calves' liver, and mounds of potatoes sprinkled with an exotic red and green substance.

The appetites of Abner Blossom and Val Sturgis appeared unimpaired, but Harlan only picked at his food, while drinking great swallows of coffee and French brandy.

"You must eat, dear Harlan," Abner advised the secretary. "There's nothing worse for grief than starvation." Abner picked up a slice of the calves' liver on a stray fork and placed it on Harlan's tongue. "Chew slowly, and thoroughly and see if you don't feel stronger, if not happier."

Abner always had such presence that few there were who ever disobeyed him. Harlan chewed therefore thoroughly and Abner took a piece of brioche and put this also in Harlan's mouth.

At first Val had been taken aback at such a peculiar performance, but then he smiled and finally laughed outright.

Abner went on feeding the bereaved Harlan and then stopped when he saw the secretary's appetite had returned.

"What would one do without friends," Harlan said throatily.

"And what will you be up to now?" Abner wondered, as a third waiter put more hash brown potatoes on every plate except Harlan's, who had waved the attendant away.

"What will I do?" Harlan wondered. "I will have to keep remembering what Cyril said to me only last week."

"And what did he say?" Abner wondered in his lofty manner while eating the hash browns energetically.

"He said, if anything should happen to me, Harlan, keep this in mind. After me in the art of photography there is really only you. And though we were in a public place, he kissed me full on the mouth." At that moment Harlan brightened a bit and refilled his glass with brandy.

"I am not at all surprised Cyril said that," Abner grew reflective. "Cyril had many sterling qualities. One of the most sterling was his ability to praise where praise was deserved, and needed. Treasure that statement, Harlan." Abner picked up one of the massive napkins not in use from a sidetable, and dried the secretary's face of tears.

"May I add my own eulogium, dear Harlan?" Val Sturgis broke in.

Harlan managed a "yes."

"It is even possible you may outstrip the Master in a special way of your own." Val spoke with conviction.

Harlan touched one of the composer's cufflinks and smiled painfully.

There was a shrieking sound of heavy wood being moved. It was the sealed coffin being taken from the apartment. At first

Harlan rose and was about to go see if everything was being properly done, when he felt a restraining hand. "Let the professionals in their field do their work, Harlan," Abner cautioned. The secretary hesitated only a moment and then sat down heavily in his chair.

A hitherto unknown waiter appeared with yet more victuals and helped everybody to more calves' liver, some grits and fried golden apples.

Abner raised his glass of spirits and everybody followed his lead in memory of the remarkable and nonpareil Cyril Vane.

The rest of the long day passed in a kind of painful, timeless half-slumber. Harlan wished he knew of some strong pill that would knock him out for a day or so. Unlike most of his generation he had never taken pills, smoked pot, or even cared much for liquor. Then as the last painful streak of light faded, he sank into a deep slumber in one of Cyril Vane's mammoth easy chairs.

He was awakened by a stream of light close to his eyes.

"Get up. I have something for you to do."

It took him what seemed like minutes even to open his eyes, and even then he could not make out anything, not even recognize the voice which was speaking to him.

"Did you hear me. Get up."

It was of course Olga Petrovna but an Olga Petrovna he had not seen before, minus her best wig, false eyelashes, and French powder and paint. Even her teeth seemed to be from a different set.

"And after tonight I don't want you sleeping here," she trumpeted.

She stepped over to the switch and turned on all the overhead lights.

He made no attempt to reply or conceal the look of dislike, even loathing on his face.

"I want the keys to his photographic studio," she spoke in a warning tone.

"I don't have them. Never have had them."

"You lie. You and he practically lived in there. Or can't you recall. I want those keys and I want them now."

"They should be in that old-fashioned roll-top desk that is in the alcove near the photography room," he finally said. All at once he wanted her to enter the room and see for herself.

"Come along and show me," she commanded.

He rose indolently, straightened his necktie and took out a pocket comb and combed his hair fastidiously, slowly.

He walked ahead of her to the roll-top desk, and rummaged among its many inside drawers.

"Here they are," he said. He handed her a string of tarnished keys.

"I want you out of this house today, and I never want to see your face again as long as I live. But wait here until I have looked through the photographic room."

"I hope you'll have the strength to leave once you've seen what's inside," Harlan thought. Then he noticed she had on only an elaborate dressing gown.

"You have something hanging from your nose, ma'am," he told her.

She snatched a handkerchief from a pocket in her robe and wiped her nose.

"Good God," he said when she was gone. "Why didn't I leave right after the funeral." He groaned.

Harlan sat motionless in Cyril's favorite armchair after she had taken the keys and gone into the forbidden chamber. "I hope it kills her," he muttered and strangely enough he managed to fall asleep.

He was awakened perhaps three hours later by moanings and cries punctuated by strings of curses which must have been in Russian or Yiddish or sometimes French.

He felt her standing over him again.

"Worse than I had expected, far worse. Pompeii, Sodom, Babylon, and I have been living under the same roof.

"And you were a party to it, a willing accomplice!" She stared at Harlan as if he would perhaps explain a thing so beyond nature, a thing which beggared the shame of the ancient cities of the plains.

"You never cried out, you never protested. I have always thought you a weak but at the same time decent young man."

"And what did you think of your husband?" Harlan responded but he did not know whether she heard him.

She had become very pale even through all the paint on her face and eyelids. She was breathing heavily, spasmodically.

"I only could take in a tiny fraction of course."

Harlan stared at her. Her emaciated breasts were rising and falling in violent arhythmic cadence. She held one beringed hand to her left side and moaned. Then she gave him a look of terror.

"Go into my room," she started to speak. "Do you hear. And in the bathroom, top shelf you'll see some medicine. It's marked 'Digitalis'. Will you go also for a tumbler of cold water?"

Harlan rose and stared at her carefully, then obeyed her.

She drank down all of the tumbler after she had taken two large purple pills from the bottle with the name Dr. Graustark, Attending Physician, in large letters.

"Shall I call the doctor, ma'am?"

"Wait a minute. Wait a minute," she sounded more civil. "Usually it passes. Usually."

"Tomorrow I will have the men come and clean out the room," she whispered.

"Those photographs are works of art," Harlan raised his voice.

She was too ill to respond.

"We will burn all of them," she said after a long pause. "More water, please."

He went to the kitchen and brought back another tumbler of water.

She drank of it like somebody exposed for hours in desert sun. After drinking she made queer sounds one would hardly recognize as coming from a fastidious rich woman. She hiccuped violently and stared now at him as if staring would reveal some of the secrets of the photography room.

"Are you certain I should not call the doctor," he went back to this.

"Absolutely sure," she replied. "And you need not stay. I told you I never want to see your face again. Never."

She kept staring at him.

"How could I have lived under the same roof and not known what was transpiring in that room all these years. Forever transpiring! Wait a minute, come closer, Harlan. I won't bite you, you fool. Let me look at you. Kneel down."

Harlan knelt down. She touched his dark face and straight black hair.

"The face does not tell all, does it? The face is a liar, and your face has lied to me. No, you do not look like one of them."

"One of who," Harlan could not control his anger.

"Like the children of Sodom," she muttered. "Degenerate, abandoned by God and man. The kingdom of forever damned."

"I am going to stay the night, Mrs. Vane," Harlan said, "whether you will it or not. I will stay to see you are all right. You will have to allow it for your own good."

"I have no good, I have nothing. The photographs have sealed off everything from me, past present future, kingdom come, all gone up in one cataclysm. Had there been a hundred stacked corpses in there it would have been a less gruesome sight."

Her color began to return. She worked the rings on her two hands frantically.

"Will you make me some strong coffee," she said in a voice more like that of a great star.

"Do you think coffee is right after your medicine?" Harlan wondered.

"When I tell you what it is I want, it is what I want, and it is of course right. So march!"

Harlan was gone so long that when he came back she had fallen asleep in his chair. She stirred and opened her eyes. She stared at the cup of hot coffee.

"Ah well, ah well," she said and received the cup. "I feel I have come back from the deepest part of the infernal kingdom. I walked down to hell and here I am sitting drinking coffee prepared by one of the participants in hell rites."

Olga Petrovna raised her coffee cup.

She tasted the brew.

"Yes, it's perfect. You have many talents, all hidden of

course from a woman who was only his spouse. How fortunate he was in having solicited your assistance for so long."

Harlan sat down in a small chair nearby. To his shame he burst into tears and sobbed.

"All the tears of the seven seas will not wash away what you are, were, and probably will go on being as you leave these premises."

Harlan wept on. She threw him a huge ornately embroidered linen handkerchief and he dried his eyes.

Abner Blossom was so engulfed in the writing of his new opera, a kind of postlude he later called it to *The Kinkajou*, that he had perhaps failed to take into account the magnitude of the scandal of Cyril Vane's funeral, and the successive scandals like intermittent explosions in a firecracker factory which came after the disgrace of the funeral.

The maenad of course of all of the tumult and the shouting was Olga Petrovna herself. Everybody said she had gone mad, but the fact was if that were so then she had always been mad, but had not had the right script by which her madness could be so completely expressed. Yet in a deeper sense the photographs and the photographic suite itself long sealed to her inquiring eye and nervous fingers had altered her faculties, disordered her senses, and unleashed in her an energy, a shameless bravado, as she went flinging to the winds of any restraint.

Other aging screen stars remembered perhaps Alla Nazimova's estimate of Olga Petrovna. Nazimova, the great Russian actress, once said when Olga had paid her a visit in her dressing room: "Always remember, my dear, that it is the firm hand on the reins and not the untamed fury of the steed that wins the day."

Olga Petrovna might have remembered the great Nazimova's words the day she flung all reason and restraint to the winds, but had she placed herself under continuous restraint there would have been no explosions of scandal and obloquy. Cyril Vane would probably have sunk into even greater oblivion than he had achieved before his death.

Scandal is the breath of fame in the United States of America. No one can be perfectly famous unless he has fallen into the glue pot. The press lives on lies, and where truth impedes its progress, truth is easily changed to headlines. The press had had lean years, and the scandal arising from the death of the old photographer-novelist brought the corpse of journalism briefly back to life.

Usually as Abner took his breakfast in his bed, Ezekiel seated himself in a chair that almost impinged on the bed itself, for Abner's deafness required proximity when one spoke to him, and Ezekiel relished booming out the latest newspaper instalments of infamy and vilification. All was of course disseminated by the servant in the interest of decency, decorum and the fitness of what one can impart.

But there was a sudden vigorous insistent ringing of the front doorbell. Ezekiel and his "master" exchanged worried glances.

"Best to answer it," Abner finally said, and rose out of the layers of bedclothes, fastened the cord of his pajama bottoms, and threw on a faded Chinese dressing gown.

He could barely make out a long sequence of whisperings, clearing of the throat, grumbling and then nervous guffaws.

A flustered but still regal Ezekiel entered the bedroom.

"Count Alexander Ilitch, Sir."

Abner gave Ezekiel a look of disbelief and irritation.

"What shall I tell him?"

"What have you told him?" Abner almost shouted.

"That you are occupied."

"Good," Abner seated himself in the little alcove next to the bedroom. "Tell him then I will see him."

Count Alexander Ilitch had passed his best years. His face which had once been superlatively handsome was now careworn and flaccid. His hair on the other hand had retained much of the color and luxuriance of his youth and gave him from a distance a look of a man in his prime.

Count Ilitch always carried a small cane which helped him keep his balance. He had a gunshot wound in his left leg sustained during a duel he had fought near the Volga River, at least according to his own story.

"This is an unexpected pleasure," Abner took the Count's hand and pressed it briefly.

"I am intruding, dear Mr. Blossom," the Count apologized.

Abner bowed faintly.

"May we speak in private?" the visitor stared at Ezekiel.

"We are in private, Count," Abner Blossom assured Ilitch.

Count Ilitch nodded, placed his cane carefully almost lovingly by the side of his chair.

Ezekiel picked the cane up despite a motion of displeasure from Count Ilitch and placed the cane just out of reach of the visitor.

"I will be brief and to the point," Count Ilitch spoke now with considerable effort. It was perhaps this effort which brought the blood to his countenance, and all at once cleared his features of the look of age. Abner Blossom's mouth opened in a kind of surprise, for Count Ilitch all at once appeared as a relatively young and extremely fetching person. His great mass of yellow hair suddenly came loose and fell indolently about his ears.

"But before I begin," Count Ilitch entreated, all the while trying to brush back his unruly shock of hair, "would it be possible for your young servant to fetch us a footstool by chance?" He pointed to his injured leg.

Ezekiel brought forth a footstool with an ornate American Indian design and placed the Count's rather dainty feet accurately and securely on the stool.

"Thank you, oh thank you," the Count cried and grasped Ezekiel's hand tightly in gratitude.

Abner now resembled in his mien more than ever that of a presiding judge.

"Mr. Blossom, you must not write the opera," the Count all at once blurted out.

There was no immediate response from Abner, but Ezekiel

paused at the door with an air of surprise, even shock at the sudden utterance of Count Ilitch. Then he hurried out.

"Must not! Cannot!" the Count repeated.

From the Count's voice now Abner recalled that his visitor had once sung in a charming male alto and had given recitals to other titled Russians living in exile.

Ezekiel returned bearing a tray with two large glasses filled with wine.

Count Ilitch's powerful right hand shook as he accepted the refreshment and he had finally to hold the glass with both hands as he thirstily sipped the wine.

"Lovely bouquet," the Count sipped again and again appreciatively. Little drops of sweat appeared on his brow and his right cheek. "But allow me to return to our problem, dear Mr. Blossom. An opera based on her husband's life – I refer of course to Madame Olga Petrovna. It would come at the worst possible time for her – Remember, dear Mr. Blossom, may I call you Abner in remembrance of your kindness to me in times past when I was honored by being invited to your sumptuous banquets here at the Enrique. . . ."

Abner Blossom raised his own glass in gracious condescension.

"Thank you," Count Ilitch whispered. "Remember, then, dear Abner," he spluttered a bit and sipped more wine, and raised his nearly empty glass to Ezekiel who immediately filled it to the brim. "Remember, then, my gracious host, that I knew Olga Petrovna in our native land, in long ages past. She was then known as Vassila. Yes, Vassila," Count Ilitch's eyes were a bit moist. "We were the dearest of friends. That is why, dear Abner, I have dared to come here today because I am her friend and compatriot although I was much younger than Vassila of course in our Russian days. I have dared to come, then, partly because of knowing her so long ago and partly because I used to be your honored guest at your banquets."

Count Ilitch now sighed heavily as he used to do when as a male alto he entertained his friends with singing arias from Tchasikowsky's lesser-known operas.

"She has sent me to you as her interlocutor!" For some

reason now Count Ilitch rose, but then remembering his wounded calf muscle he sat abruptly down.

"Vassila, pardon me, I mean Olga Petrovna begs you on bended knee," Count Ilitch concluded his request, and almost feverishly finished his second glass of wine, again filled to overflowing by the attentive Ezekiel.

Gazing over at his employer, for a moment Ezekiel thought that Abner had fallen asleep for his employer had his eyes closed tightly to the added discomfiture of Count Ilitch.

"We once spent an entire long evening together on the Volga," Count Ilitch spoke so low at that moment that Abner Blossom could not possibly have heard him, and had kept in any case his eyes tightly closed.

"I greatly appreciate your taking time from your own pressing affairs to come here, Count Ilitch, all on behalf of our dear friend Olga Petrovna, or as you called her of yore, Vassila. . . . But see here –" Abner now opened both his eyes widely – "I cannot even acknowledge I have heard such a request on your part or hers."

"Cannot?" Count Ilitch asked in an amazed theatrical tone, and again Abner Blossom imagined he could hear the Count's male alto voice in recital.

"Cannot, will not, never shall countenance such a request, even when it comes from so prepossessing, so winsome, so elegant and manly a gentleman as yourself, Count Ilitch. I have always admired you. I have always wanted to be of service to you now and in the future. But I cannot help you because in the first place there is no such opera in progress."

"No such opera," Count Ilitch asked hopefully.

"None whatsoever. Certainly, dear Count, none based on the life of – you did call her Vassila I believe. No such opera based on Vassila's life or that of her dead and departed spouse exists!"

Count Ilitch fell back in his chair with stunned relief.

"There is however an opera. Make no mistake about that. But it concerns other parties. And to be frank, to speak openly as I can to a dear friend such as yourself. . . ."

As Abner Blossom hesitated, the Count pushed forward in

his chair with deep attention, and his coiffure now became totally disarranged and fell almost to his shoulders.

"I have found Vassila and her husband already too operatic for my talent to do them justice. They are already too grand. There would be no room for my talent with such personages. And in the case of Vassila . . ."

"Olga, please say Olga," Count Ilitch persisted now.

"Olga or Vassila, and please forgive me, Count, is despite many sterling qualities, a bit on the vulgar side."

Strange to say, Count Ilitch nodded now as if the stricture he had just heard against Olga was entirely in accord with his own feelings.

"Alas, alas," Count Ilitch said, and then broke into several phrases in Russian. At this moment he rose and bowed deeply.

Abner Blossom also now rose, and looked up into the face of his visitor, who being over six feet four in height, appeared indeed far away.

"Let me say in conclusion, dear Count," Abner no longer attempted to look up into a countenance so far away, "the personages in my opera may have originally been based on actual human beings, or even on one gentleman and lady in particular. But both my libretto found by chance or fate in the Blind Cat night club, and my music have completely transmuted whatever characters they may have originally been based on. Call it alchemy, dear Count. There is in the end only my music and my words. Otherwise, dear Count Ilitch, hundreds of unfaithful married men and their neglected spouses could send ambassadors here to interdict my work and my opera."

All at once Count Ilitch perhaps by reason of Abner's speech or by reason of the excessive amount of wine he had drunk, looked much reduced in height. Almost as low of stature as Abner Blossom.

"The whole world, Mr. Blossom, will have to judge then who the characters in your opera are! I have fulfilled my mission as Olga Petrovna's ambassador and interlocutor here today. And let us not diminish your talent as a great composer and librettist. No, no, dear Abner. But by the very nature of your genius, sir, it will be clear to the audience who the characters are in real life. I would hope though that you might make any changes not inconsistent with your artistic principles and therefore perhaps postpone the première of the opera until dear Vassila or Olga has passed from the scene."

"Vassila, or Olga Petrovna, dear Count, will never pass away in my opinion. Women like her never die! And I cannot wait until the next century. My decision is therefore final, Count, and I bid you good morning."

"I leave you therefore, dear Mr. Blossom," the caller spoke calmly even if brokenhearted. "I say I leave you, a keenly disappointed and aggrieved man." Here Count Ilitch having reached his full height bent down low and kissed Abner Blossom rather loudly on both the composer's cheeks.

"And my deepest gratitude to you for having received me so beneficently, so graciously. . . ."

Count Ilitch now turned somewhat helplessly to Ezekiel Loomis, who handed him his gold-tipped cane.

Having passed out of earshot of his host, Count Ilitch turned his full attention to Ezekiel Loomis, whose own rather regal bearing had gradually been impressing itself on the Russian ambassador.

"Allow me to say, dear sir," he addressed the servant, "I have met with one of the greatest defeats of my career."

Seeing his wine glass still half-filled, the Count seized it and said, "May I drink to your health and happiness, young man. And may I say it without impertinence or condescension, dear Ezekiel Loomis, that I see in you the future of this American nation."

Count Ilitch drank thirstily and noisily, handed his empty glass to Ezekiel, and hurried out brandishing in the air his gold-tipped cane.

The death of Cyril Vane was to have a lasting effect on many persons, but on none more deeply than Abner Blossom.

Abner had long prided himself on being always above time and tide, unscathed by the slings and arrows of nearly all fortune, and rising like the phoenix from the ashes of his many defeats as a composer. Indeed he had made a career of turning his failures into successes. None of his operas had been well received, but scandal and a vocal minority of supporters had turned them into scandalous triumphs.

But the death of Cyril Vane struck him a deeper blow than the bricks and jeers of the critics and the unthinking public. Abner felt for one thing old. Cyril Vane might have been his somewhat young father, and of course had been however fleetingly his lover.

"There is now no one who is older than me!" Abner had exclaimed to a dozing Ezekiel Loomis, who started a bit from his chair, ashamed he had fallen off to sleep while his employer was addressing him.

Yes, if Harlan Yost had all at once after the death of Cyril Vane, seen himself as a middle-aged man with a suddenly noticeable swarthy complexion and no real accomplishments in life, Abner Blossom saw himself now perhaps not as an ancient (which Cyril Vane most certainly had been) but as dreadfully unmistakenly superlatively old, if somewhat well-preserved despite his cruel baldness and growing deafness. But his genius was not old, he consoled himself. His muse was ever young and ceaselessly productive.

"Ezekiel," he beckoned his attendant to draw near. "Do I look horribly venerable, do you think?"

Ezekiel bent down to say something, and Abner all at once kissed the servant deferentially on his brow.

Ezekiel drew back in surprise and gave forth a kind of snorting sound.

It took some moments then for both employer and servant to recover themselves and go back to their old decorum. But just prior to leaving the room to return to the kitchen, Ezekiel cleared his throat and said: "Not old, Mr. Blossom, *grand* is more like it, I believe."

Abner gazed after the retreating figure of Ezekiel, and once he had left the room Abner sat as if meditating on what his hired man had just said.

Then Abner raised his voice to say: "I will write my opera as only I can and will brook no interference from Russian noblemen. Let Olga Petrovna do her worst. Let her scalp me if she dare. That opera will be given to my public and given with no strings attached. It will be my voice, my music, my words. Cyril Vane and Olga Petrovna should be flattered I have chosen them to live on in my music. Let her do her damndest do you hear, Zeke. Her damndest!"

"I hear you, sir," Ezekiel's voice rose above the sound of running water and cups being washed and scalded. Drying his hands quickly, Ezekiel strode into the living room where Abner was talking out loud still.

"I hope you didn't let Count Ilitch upset you, Mr. Blossom," Ezekiel began. "You surely would not let a little aristocrat from the Volga prevent you from finishing your great opera!"

Abner had never heard Ezekiel speak so urgently, almost rapturously. He turned his full gaze on his servant.

"There have been times, Ezekiel, when I thought my powers had waned. I will be truthful. Count Ilitch did get to me a bit."

"But the opera, dear Mr. Blossom, must go forward!"

Abner smiled and closed his eyes.

"Oh, don't you worry. I will. Olga, or as Count Ilitch calls her Vassila, may scalp me, let her. She can't very well tear down the opera house or kill all the singers or destroy the score."

Here Abner Blossom produced the bulky already badly stained libretto and waved it in the air.

"Let Olga Petrovna do her damndest to stop my music . . . but let me tell you something, Ezekiel, she longs for infamy, just as her late husband longed for forbidden pleasure. She would be in seventh heaven if my opera would let the whole world know she is its heroine. She would relish her disgrace and notoriety. It would be the sweetest chapter in her long career of playing second fiddle to Cyril Vane. She would glory in infamy, revel in full scale obloquy!"

Both men were silent for a while.

"The Count will of course tell her that the opera is going forward, and that without the shadow of a doubt it concerns her and her late spouse, and that I stand firm and unshakable."

His face wreathed in broad smiles, grinning widely, showing all of his wonderfully white teeth adorned with gold, Ezekiel returned uplifted and joyous to his own quarters.

Valentine Sturgis was capable of being jealous where Luigi was concerned, jealous even of inanimate objects which his beloved cared for. An example was a thumbed, well-worn book in Italian titled *Elegia di Madonna Fiammetta*. Luigi read the book constantly. When his lover was absent Val would leaf through the pages of the book, but his Italian was too inadequate for him to understand much of it. But on the last page he found in Luigi's own handwriting the English words: "When love has reached its highest perfection, it can only begin to decline and like the sun set in darkness."

The sentence haunted Val from then on. He even thought of setting the words to music, for he felt they contained some urgent prophesy. At times he would console himself that the sentence must after all be only a translation from *Madonna Fiammetta*, and not anything which Luigi thought and felt.

Once as they lay in bed together in the early morning hours, Val with some trepidation inquired: "What kind of a book is that you are reading from all the time, Luigi?"

He could hear Luigi swallowing convulsively, which he always did when something upset him. When there was no answer, Val nudged him gently, then when there was still no response, he kissed Luigi on his ear lobe, and let his hand slide down to his thigh.

"A book about unrequited love," Luigi responded at last and took Val's hand tightly in his.

"Do you still love me?" Val wondered.

"Can you doubt it?" Luigi responded quickly.

"I would die if you did not," Val choked out.

"No, dear friend," Luigi spoke now all at once in a heavy Sicilian accent. "You would get over it. You would forget me. You would not be like Madonna Fiammetta in the story who wasted away from love."

And from the time he had looked into the Italian love story, a gripping uneasiness, a freezing terror took hold of Val. What increased his foreboding was the fact that Luigi was kinder, more loving, more considerate to him than ever before.

"He is going to leave me, and I will die like Madonna Fiammetta," Val would say to himself. Once while shaving and looking at himself carefully in the mirror all at once he noticed with another kind of sickness that a few gray hairs were visible in his sideburns. The razor almost slipped out of his hand.

One night when neither of them could sleep, Luigi got up and opened the story of Fiammetta and began reading aloud in Italian. The music of the language was only matched by the beauty of Luigi's voice.

"Could you just sing some of it to me," Val suggested.

"For you I would sing all of it. For you I would be an angel pouring out my words for you through eternity." Luigi spoke jokingly but with feeling none the less.

Val sat up in bed and listened as Luigi improvised melodies as he read from the Italian love story.

Each day from then on when Val would return from his various undertakings he would expect to see a note like the one Hugh had once left behind, bidding him farewell, and signed Luigi.

But nothing happened. Their love, if it did not increase, remained on the same unshakable course of passion, tenderness and mutual need.

When singing in his church choir Val had often wondered if the peace and perfection of paradise might not finally become unendurable by its very perfection and bliss. But then he could only think of his own love for Luigi. So long as he could hold him in his arms, touch his hyacinthine hair with his fingers, and feel the pulse and vibration of his sex, this was a paradise that had no flaw, no flagging of joy. He was in the empyrean, had reached the promised land.

If Val Sturgis and Luigi lived in a heaven of their own, Francis X. Beauregard felt himself plunged into the most stygian of infernos. In this hell he had but one thought and felt only one desire – Luigi. He wearied his old friends of the silent and early talking films by breaking into diatribes against the runaway Sicilian, diatribes followed by almost nauseous descriptions of the details of his love for the young Sicilian. Caught up in spite of themselves in this chronicle of disappointed love, the old stars would sit by the hour listening to Francis' account of his worship of Luigi.

Beauregard ordered even more expensive imported dressing gowns, would parade about in them staring at himself in the ceiling-high mirrors. He summoned the most expensive hair stylist in Manhattan who worked on him for hours, relining his eyebrows, tinting his hair (which surprisingly enough had few strands of gray) and finishing by praising in shameless flattery Francis' remaining good looks, his ageless skin and firm musculature.

More Chinese masseurs came and went, inflicting at times by his own command painful adjustments of muscle, tendon and bone.

Then in the evening, attended by a driver and two servants, Francis would spin through the deserted back streets of Brooklyn with its long-closed mansions whose ceilings sported great chandeliers still hanging like beacons commemorating a once splendid, certainly much happier and grander epoch.

"Unless I can bring him back, I will perish," he told an attentive and smitten young Guatemalan youth, who doted on his employer's every whim and command.

He hired detectives, paid them ridiculously overpriced fees, placed puzzlingly ambiguous ads in magazines read only by rich pederasts, even one evening like some dope-ridden boy he indulged in writing graffiti on the walls of a museum and on sidewalks, with such banal messages as *Luigi, All is forgiven but nothing forgotten, come home and write your own ticket, take all I have and own, it is yours. Francis X.*

He now began driving in one of his 1920s antique autos through streets deserted at the hour he chose, and as he wandered with his paid companions he would marvel at the splendid wrecks of the mansions in Brooklyn. Like him, he thought, they were too grand, too beautiful, too remote to be considered as existing in the living present. He wept convulsively at having outlived everything, even his own all-consuming love of himself.

Yet love had not surrendered him, for his love of a wild, untamed, cruel and unattainable Sicilian youth, who like him, different though he was, belonged somehow to the kingdom of the dead. Luigi's heart, whatever had crushed it, no longer beat in cadence with this time and world. Not for nothing were Francis X. and Luigi chalked up together by destiny, brought always somehow again together, by some fluke of fate.

One night the young Guatemalan asked to see Francis X.'s palm. "You read palms?" the choked voice of the screen actor came from behind a scarf which covered all of his face but his pale blue eyes.

"He is coming back to you," the Guatemalan told him. "Soon," the servant added in a high falsetto. "*Muy pronto.*"

Certain changes in Luigi's behavior became a source of worry to Val Sturgis, but he was so absorbed in writing new songs and choral works based on, in fact, the wonderful things Luigi said to him, the pathetically beautiful story of Madonna Fiammetta, and the kind of rapturous love Luigi had brought to him that he put aside any fleeting concern and worry.

After all, he reflected, Luigi's childhood and early youth were made unendurable by the cruelty of his stepfather who beat him remorselessly, by poverty and deprivation of every kind, and, finally owning to his extreme attractiveness, by being loved to the point of worship by his different paramours.

But his reflections added up to nothing. Luigi was undergoing some drastic change for the worse. He often stayed up all night, praying to a tiny image of some saint (he refused to tell Val the name of the holy one), and often sitting with his eyes unfocused and filmy, gazing at the void.

The final climax came one stormy winter night, when the windows rattled, and the north-west wind invaded their sleeping room with hurricane-like force.

It was then that Val Sturgis began worrying about himself as much as he worried about his friend. For that night unable to sleep he saw that Luigi had risen and was standing in the middle of the room, the rapt expression in his eyes, his entire body moving in a kind of violent succession of tremors, his arms rising toward the ceiling when, yes, Val would swear it was what he saw, Luigi all at once rose upward toward the ceiling like some great sea bird.

Val Sturgis in his fright tumbled out of bed and lay sprawled on the floor looking upward at what he was sure could not be occuring. He had read about levitation, but had never believed even St. Theresa had accomplished the miracle. But how was he to explain what he saw? Above him the long black hair and the light clothing of his loved one moved like the feathers of a hawk. But the expression in that bird's eyes was vacuous, dead.

Without warning a cry escaped from Val's mouth as he crouched in terror on the floor. The cry brought a change of expression in the ascending youth, his eyes came alive and focused about him, his arms flailed violently and his knees raised toward his belly. Looking down at that moment he saw Val in an attitude of desperation. Luigi let out a cry also as if he too was viewing something beyond the realm of nature. As he cried he began descending violently and fell close to the outstretched hands of Val. The two young men clasped one another in their arms.

It was Luigi's turn now to comfort Val. He smoothed his

hair, rubbed his temples, and kissed him repeatedly.

"What have I seen – you tell me – what has been happening?" or some such words came out of Val's mouth pressed tight against Luigi's chest. For answer, Luigi only held him more tightly to him.

The next morning, dressed very formally with a tie and jacket, Luigi was drinking his morning brew, while Val haggard and attired only in his pajamas and a robe, stared away from his lover, and every so often would cough hoarsely to disguise his sobs.

"I was taught it first in Sicily," Luigi began without preamble, like a sleepwalker who has found the person he has been searching for, a person who has waited many nights perhaps, months for an explanation of the mystery.

"A monk and a nun taught me. It came to me, they said, as effortlessly as a young bird nudged out of his nest by its parent finally takes off in flight in the air. At the same time, when I told this to my Abbot, the Abbot I betrayed," he added with a kind of rage, "My Abbot said, 'Luigi, did you ever think that the person who sees you levitate may only be thinking he sees what you wish him to.' 'No, Father,' I replied. 'I know I do levitate, and I do not think I even desire to.'"

Whether Luigi had levitated or not, or Val Sturgis (who had very little religious belief or knowledge of such phenomena) merely thought he saw his friend levitate, the strange event cast a chill upon their love. It did not end Val's love for Luigi, far from it. But it made his love like the word "elegy" in the story of Madonna Fiammetta, a vigil of tenderness and sorrow, a watch as at a death-bed.

As Val was later to tell Abner Blossom (who listened to the whole account with a kind of shocked disbelief and unease), "I annointed him with my love for his new and final voyage, and I saw as I held his hand that he returned my love by every fibre of his being."

One morning when the weather had cleared and the two friends were listening to some early Italian music, the Guatemalan servant of Francis X. Beauregard walked into the room unannounced. Luigi stood up in a shock similar to that which Val Sturgis had demonstrated when he saw Luigi levitate.

The Guatemalan asked (in Spanish) to be pardoned for his intrusion and extended a letter to Luigi.

Luigi handed the letter only half-read to Val. It read:

Francis X. Beauregard has suffered a life-threatening stroke. He keeps asking for you. Can you come at once? He may not last out the day according to medical opinion.

It was signed but the signature was indecipherable.

"Will you let me go. Please say what you wish. I will not go if you forbid it," Luigi turned to Val.

Val Sturgis struggled with himself. This mysterious message, like the nightmare of seeing Luigi levitate, resembled the far-off sound of bells tolling the end of his happiness, his very life.

"For a friend who loves you," Val struggled to get the words out, "you must go of course."

The Guatemalan smiled broadly, and bowed, then seeing one of the dainties Abner Blossom had sent a few days ago, a kind of chocolate opera cream, he snatched it and put it in his mouth and accompanied a bereft Luigi from the room, who finally looking back, blew a delicate kind of kiss with his right hand at a transfixed Val Sturgis.

"You will be in for a surprise," the Guatemalan spoke now in rather more fluent English than Luigi remembered him speaking earlier. "We are going in a police squad car," he added.

Seeing a small cafe open, the Guatemalan popped in and out before Luigi could respond, returning with a paper cup full of fruit juice. He produced then from his brand-new green jacket pocket a tiny Florentine pill-box. Taking out a pill, he extended it cautiously to Luigi. "Mr. Francis X. wanted you to take this." Pausing he added "Against sorrow."

Luigi stared at the pill, stared at the Guatemalan. Then putting the pill on his tongue he crushed and swallowed it. "If I die," he remarked to his guide, "it won't be the first time."

They laughed together mournfully.

Lieutenant McIntosh got out of the squad car when he saw the two approaching. He identified himself and gave a rather long speech which Luigi could barely follow but which informed him that owing to Mr. Francis X.'s many kindnesses and support to the police force, he was glad to be able to convey one of the great actor's friends for a last meeting and farewell.

"Will I be able to . . ." but Luigi did not finish, being just then helped by the lieutenant into the back seat with the Guatemalan messenger.

"Oh how long a ride that is from Grove Street, Manhattan to the further reaches of mysterious Brooklyn and its forsaken mansions," Luigi mumbled to himself.

Whether it was the pill he had taken or the weight of sorrow, Luigi could remember nothing until he saw the quantity of straw strewn about the deserted streets and sidewalks, the straw reaching onto the steps of the mansion, straw everywhere and quiet.

"*Paglia, paglia,*" Luigi finally spoke. The officer stared at him closely as he helped him get out of the squad car. The officer then turned to the Guatemalan and said something.

The next thing Luigi remembered he was standing in front of the long bed in the center of the room they named the Crocus Room, it was so yellow. But Luigi was unable to see who was lying in the bed by reason of such an assemblage of priests, obviously all of high rank, and the presence everywhere of a number of police officers.

Even more oppressive was the choking smell of incense. The straw, the incense, the thought that there must be actual crocuses somewhere, and the fact that the pallid yellow light was dimming constantly as if the sun itself had disintegrated around them, stupefied him. But at last the concourse of priests in their fearful black robes and hanging crucifixes made a path for him. He stood in front of his idol, and then knelt down.

Francis X. Beauregard was nearly unrecognizable, but his right hand which he extended painfully to Luigi was certainly his, although so wasted and pale as was every other part of the flesh that was visible.

"In time, thank fortune, in time," he heard Francis' voice but a voice that seemed to come from rooms away, stifled perhaps too by straw and incense and crocus light.

"I will wait for you, Luigi," Francis said, "till the end of time."

Luigi placed his head down on the sick man's bed, and felt the familiar caresses from the dying actor's fingers.

"Did you hear me?" Francis inquired. "I will wait for you till time has ended."

The priests now moved through all the clouds of incense, toward the bed, toward Luigi. He felt himself pulled away from his idol, his friend. He felt himself sink back in other strong unfeeling but not as yet cruel hands as when they had beaten him for running away from his uncle in Sicily. He felt he heard the rawhide again descending on him, but this was the rawhide of death, blinding him with its leather bite, the death of the idol he had worshipped.

Val Sturgis would later tell Abner Blossom, "I hardly dared breathe when he finally came back from Francis X. Beauregard."

"Don't talk in riddles." Abner Blossom was as severe as he always was when someone spoke out of pure anguish or passion.

"He was changed, totally changed," Val Sturgis went on, but he omitted nearly everything he really had seen or felt. He told no one what transpired after Luigi was freed from Francis X. Beauregard.

Freed?

Val would sit at night in his own sprawling loft when it was all over and reflect, would jot down notes, real notes for the pianoforte. He would finally, he knew, write something out of his own love and loss.

Luigi had allowed Val to hold him, to caress him, to kiss him with a fearful, famined, unappeaseable frenzy.

They lay down for awhile on the floor.

"You will never, never. . . ."

"What?" Luigi stirred angrily in the fierce embrace of his lover.

"Don't say it," Luigi put his hand over Val's mouth. "Refrain."

"If you leave I will. . . ."

Luigi again closed Val's mouth painfully. His fingers felt like they had been handling ashes.

Unlike the funeral of Cyril Vane, regarded by the press as in the worst of taste, and of a bad taste inconsistent even with its own bad taste, the majestic funeral of Francis X. Beauregard in one of the City's great cathedrals drew dignitaries from across the nation and from abroad. The American public seldom remembers anybody or anything which is not at that very moment pouring out tons of print, money and acclaim. Francis X. belonged to a world which had disappeared so long ago that they who did recall him in his prime were often ashamed to admit they knew him lest the new America would realize they too belonged to the catacombs and vicissitudes of oblivion.

Luigi was too shaken, too ill actually to attend the funeral, and the great princes of the Church who were to officiate were, it was said, greatly relieved the young friend of the deceased would not make his presence known.

Luigi ran a high fever, and finally he permitted Val to summon a physician. The doctor came, indifferently felt the patient's pulse, listened to his chest, and handed Val a box of capsules.

"Keep him warm, bathe his forehead frequently." The doctor's voice trailed off as the final words came: "And call this public number if he should worsen."

After the doctor left Luigi laughed boisterously at the old medic's words, and Val felt some trifle of encouragement.

But Val's own purgatory was now to begin.

Often in the middle of the night Val would be awakened by Luigi talking deliriously in his sleep, and Val was able to pick up out of the words in Sicilian the name Francis, Francis. Val would nudge him then and Luigi would open his eyes, smile and kiss his friend.

One night after listening to Luigi mumble for half the night in his native language, Val heard Luigi say in English, "I can't leave for a short time yet."

Those nights became more frenzied, and for Val, were long sleepless torments. He would often awaken and find Luigi gone from his side. Then looking about he would see his friend acting like a sleepwalker, finally to take his stand at the one huge window of the room to look out vacantly into the extinct caverns of the sleeping city, and calling softly, "Francis, Francis, where are you?"

Val rushed up to Luigi and shook him. Coming out of his rapt state, Luigi turned savagely on the composer and struck him across the face. Then roused and becoming fully awake, Luigi grieved over what he had done, wept, apologized, and took Val in his arms and covered his face and brow with kisses.

"But I knew," Val would later tell those who would care to listen, "I knew he was going away from me. I knew too he had never belonged to me, and yet I had belonged only to him. Out of all and everybody I had met or been with, Luigi was the only other soul I belonged with, and he desired only one thing, to leave me. His vocation was desertion."

One terrible night, it was the last one, Val would waken many times, and find Luigi gone from his side. He would call him then, and Luigi would patiently come back and lie beside him. This occured at least ten times during the last night they were together.

About dawn Val awakened, and saw there was nobody in the room. He called. Then he rose and searched everywhere in the apartment. But what finally caught his eye – the big window was wide open.

Then from below in the street he heard the noise of voices

raised, the shriek of a police car, hoarse male shouts, tumult, the sick scream of brakes.

He looked down. A searchlight illuminated the stark message.

He recognized his own bathrobe draped over the only one he had ever loved, and whom now he saw he had lost forever.

A policeman looked up at the open window. Someone blew a whistle.

Val Sturgis slipped to the floor, his hands grasping tightly the window sill, then the hands relaxed, and he slipped down into an unconsciousness almost as profound as that which had enveloped Luigi Cervo forever.

"A concatenation of events!" Abner Blossom scurried around his studio repeating this phrase so that one would have thought he had invented both the long word and the phrase it found itself in.

"Zeke! Zeke!" he would call in a frenzy, "are you on that private phone again? Come here this instant."

Ezekiel spent long hours, according to Abner, talking to his great aunt Beth in Harlem. He once overheard one of the conversations. He was not appalled but fascinated by what he heard. For all that Zeke told Beth was a meticulous, yes, punctilious retelling of the events of the week. "Mr. Blossom's new opera, let me tell you, titled *Cock Crow*, has been completely financed by a great Maecenas, and is in rehearsal. Somewhere in Brooklyn, near the Brooklyn bridge, is a decayed amphitheater, to use Mr. Blossom's term, a very huge building once used for prize fights and wrestling matches and then with the arrival of the Latinos, cockfights, but many years ago when Manhattan as the late Cyril Vane would have described her, when she was a flowering meadow with its secret drinking gardens, in that very amphitheater, the divine Jeanne Eagles, the most beautiful woman next to Greta Garbo probably who ever appeared on the silent screen – Miss Eagles in that very amphitheater, yes, Jeanne Eagles met in a secret rendezvous the heartcrusher of his epoch, Jack Gilbert. They were protected in their secret meeting by four armed guards. Yes, oh yes he is unnerved Mr. Blossom is, over one of the greatest scandals to become public, the death of both Francis X. Beauregard and his secret amour, the young Sicilian Luigi Cervo. And the subsequent almost fatal illness of Abner Blossom's protégé, the gifted forthcoming master of ballads and cantatas, Val Sturgis, from Kentucky."

"My heart aches for you," Abner Blossom had written Val on one of his ornate notepapers. "You must hold out! I will visit you in hospital tomorrow. Please remember you are loved, adored by many, worshipped by one at least, Yours ever, A.B."

The rumor was that Val Sturgis had also attempted suicide shortly after the inquest into the death of Luigi, the Chimney Swift.

Several papers had been handed to Val by lawyers and court stenographers during the inquest. One question indeed had been, "What was the significance of your friend being called the Chimney Swift?"

A court doctor had been called and Val had been taken to an adjoining room for examination.

Returning alone, the doctor had told the presiding officer at the inquest that Mr. Sturgis was neither mentally nor physically able to continue testifying.

The inquest was brought to a close, and the result when later made public was: Suicide by leaping from the fifth story of a West Side Apartment. Family or place, and date of birth unknown.

Another link in the concatenation was also legal. Olga Petrovna had somehow got possession of the libretto for *Cock Crow*, and had recognized herself in the principal female role, a woman who Demeter-like wanders the earth (Manhattan) in search of Proserpine, (in the libretto the countless numbers of young black males whom her late husband worshipped, adored, photographed and held close in rapture).

It was as though the acerbic tones of Abner Blossom

himself drifted over to her. Olga Petrovna had remembered once having eavesdropped on Cyril and Abner speaking privately together. Abner's voice came back to her now as clearly as if he were standing before her: "In America money triumphs even over wronged wives."

So much money had already been put into the forthcoming opera, that the lawyers representing Olga Petrovna advised her finally she could not possibly win a case against the librettist and the composer (both being actually Abner Blossom himself) and that if she sued Abner for libel her own name would be further blackened.

Enraged by such spineless surrender, Olga Petrovna went from one famous attorney to another, finally coming up with Horatio Vinter who charged her a fee just for listening to her charges, a fee which would have kept her in food and drink and new gowns for several months of the year. And in the end all Mr. Vinter would tell her was he would watch and wait and keep her informed.

Meanwhile the opera was in rehearsal and, as a local tabloid put it, without one white face in the cast, orchestra or even box office. Another tabloid weeks before *Cock Crow* would première blazoned on its front page

BLACK OPERA TO STUN WHITE WORLD.

There came a slight calm and letup in all the frenzied never-ending rehearsals, the changes in the score, the endless arguments with the conductor and leading soloists, and Abner Blossom stole away unobserved to see Valentine Sturgis.

Val smiled faintly as Abner was ushered in by Val's new room-mate, a young saxophonist from Alabama who had hopes of rising in the music world.

"Your own color is back," Abner complimented Val, who getting up from his bed, shook Abner's hand and hugged him lengthily.

"Aren't you going to introduce me to the gentleman who

guided me in?" Abner broke away from Val's embrace.

"Kenny," Val raised his voice, "meet Mr. Blossom, our greatest opera composer."

Abner gave one of his more splendid bows to the saxophonist, who shook the old man's hand painfully.

But Abner Blossom's eye had wandered to the window from which, according to the news stories, Luigi Cervo had leapt to his death.

"You'll have a cup of tea, I hope! Ken has gone to the trouble of preparing us a little snack also," Val broke into Abner's musings.

Both Abner Blossom's friends and his enemies had often said of him: "He never refuses food or praise."

Abner nodded with his indulgent bow, and Ken brought in a sumptuous repast.

Munching assiduously, Abner began: "You will write even greater songs, Val, with more cantatas, and finally, now don't interrupt me, *you* will write an opera."

Val Sturgis sighed. He felt too debilitated even to inscribe his own name at that moment. But he knew how much Abner detested tears, even sighs. Yet the older man, looking about him, felt something in the room that was a nullification of his own dictum never to consult the heart. There was sorrow and loss and longing and unappeasable grief in every corner of the room.

Abner accepted another Parker House roll from Kenny. "You both have only to call me when I am needed," Abner got out between mouthfuls. Pausing a moment, he went on, "And who did you say baked the Parker House rolls, for I can taste they're not store bought." Ken blushed and fidgeted, acknowledging he was the cook, and Val began to recover a little of his old aplomb and gaiety.

"Please, Mr Blossom, tell us about the production of *Cock Crow*," Ken said beginning to recover a bit from the shock of meeting the composer.

Abner warmed to the subject. "You boys knew of course Olga Petrovna is trying to stop the opera from being put on." He reached for another hot roll.

Abner now launched into an elaborate recital of all the

146

problems, misunderstandings, trivialities, frustrations, and even free-for-alls of every kind that surround the birth of an opera, ending with the final exhaustion, headache, depression and the classic blues that are meted out to genius.

"But, see here," the old man exclaimed as he shook some crumbs off his ever-expanding stomach, "You have to remember, I am above all else a soldier and a fighter. For an artist never surrenders, never has in his possession the white flag. A composer, or even what is slightly lower on the scale, a writer, shall we say, he never surrenders. He is the fighting man forever. Battles are his life blood and life energy. Fight! Struggle! Engage in mortal hand-to-hand combat. And then soar upward!" Abner fell back in his chair and shook his head in delight at his own words, picked up another roll and stuffed it almost whole into his mouth.

Val felt a great surge of energy coming from the veteran of so many skirmishes and battles, and for the first time in many days the pain of losing Luigi abated to a small degree, as if the sun had partially burst forth in the Manhattan cloud-ridden sky.

In the midst of those tumultuous rehearsals for *Cock Crow*, the telephone had been taken off the hook while in a corner, behind a frayed oriental screen, Abner Blossom was working in feverish haste over the score and libretto. Ezekiel entered unannounced carrying in on its long wire the special private telephone.

"Yes?" Abner stared balefully at his servant.

"For you, sir. A personal call this time."

"Zeke," the frantic composer shouted causing his spectacles to slip down from his nose. "How many times must I impress upon you there are to be no phone calls!"

"But it's Mr. Nigel Langtree, calling from San Diego, sir."

And the servant lifted his eyes hopelessly to the ceiling as he tried to hand over the telephone to the composer.

"Nigel Langtree," Abner gave a faint gasp. "But I thought he died in that car crash all the papers put on the front page."

Shaking his head majestically, Ezekiel almost pushed the telephone now into the composer's hands.

"But certainly, Zeke, I read Nigel perished in an inferno of a racing car crash," Blossom boomed in his deaf-man's voice.

Placing his fingers over his lips, Ezekiel corrected his employer in faint whispers:

"It was Nigel's friend Freddy, the stock-car racer, who died, sir. Mr. Nigel Langtree is just out of the hospital in San Diego. He insists on speaking to you."

Nodding violently, Abner spoke into the mouthpiece:

"I just heard all you said, Abner," came the familiar voice of the celebrated young British film director. "No, no, dear Abner, I am not calling from the other shore. I've been in town for some time but could never reach you on the telephone."

Abner almost began to coo over the phone, while Ezekiel stood with pained fortitude, waiting to be dismissed, and then finally left the room without permission.

"Of course you can come, Nigel," Abner's voice drifted out to the buttery where Ezekiel was alternately shaking his head and quietly chuckling. "But when you come, for heaven's sake, don't bring anybody with you. And of course *Cock Crow* will be a smash, you certainly know at this stage in my career, I dare not, I cannot fail."

At the conclusion of the phone call, Ezekiel came into the room to carry back the phone to the adjoining room.

"Didn't we agree, Zeke, there were to be absolutely no phone calls," Abner began.

"Mr. Nigel Langtree is the exception that proves the rule, wouldn't you say, sir?"

Abner grinned broadly.

"Fancy me thinking Nigel had died in that racing car crash."

"It was Mr. Langtree's close friend, sir, Freddy, who died in the crash. The Venezuelan speed-car king Mr. Langtree was so taken with, you recall. Why, they were both here as your guests time after time."

"Go on," Mr. Blossom's expression seemed to indicate.

"The young friend was smashed to pieces in the wreck, Mr. Blossom. They carried his remains away in bushel baskets, I read, and your Nigel, sir, they took one look at him when they pulled him from the burning exploding wreck, and from then on the film director lay between two worlds for months, and yet after all the medics, specialists, nurses and priests had said farewell and goodbye to him, lo and behold one bright sun-shiney morning in San Diego, Nigel Langtree sits up in bed, rubs his eyes, and orders a pot of tea with french toast sprinkled with brown sugar!"

"Thank God, Ezekiel. And my gratitude to you for letting Mr. Langtree speak to me. As usual, Zeke, you are always right."

And a few hours later, Mr. Nigel Langtree entered the Hotel Enrique in person, a little like one of the film stars he was always directing, a bit haughty, if not condescending (he had condescended to America now for most of his life, being, as he always said he was, a true-blue Englishman). He strode up to Abner and took the old composer in his arms and held him tight.

"My own ribs, Abner, are practically pure plastic. I lost a kidney, my spleen, and my liver they thought would never function again for all the holes, and my leg" (here he pulled up his pant legs to reveal fearful scars) "is as good as wooden, but, Abner, I wanted to live if only to see you again!"

Abner continued to melt, continued to grin, and continued to sing praises of Nigel Langtree for his life, his work, and his love.

"But don't tell me you have come back to be a fifth wheel again for all those 98-year-old film beauties you are always making Grade B films of."

"All over," Nigel sat down, "at least all over for now," he finished as he accepted the usual king-sized cup of coffee from Ezekiel's hand, and sipping murmured "mmm" and "thank you" to the servant.

"Look here, Nigel," Abner began in his confidential tone, "I have just the party for you, for I recall you are the biggest complainer about lonesomeness I ever met."

There was a sudden silence.

"Let me say something here," Nigel began and put down the coffee cup with a timing which recalled his direction of many of the film queens of the past fifty years, "let me remind you, Abner, if I need to, my dearest friend of all my dearest friends ever, Freddy, is gone."

Abner looked away and waited.

"The gods were jealous of us, Abner. Spiteful, malcontent, determined to take one of us. We were much too happy. Why they left me, dear friend, I can't say."

"They left you because you're a genius on celluloid no doubt."

Nigel was silent, then sipped his coffee.

"I can tell you are about to command me to do something again, sweetheart," Nigel spoke craftily.

"I have a friend who has also lost his dearest friend," Abner admitted.

"You're sending me out today before I've got settled again in Manhattan, you mean."

"He's as talented as you are, this friend, but of course not yet known. Composes the finest songs since probably Stephen Collins Foster."

"Name and address," Nigel spoke acidly.

Very much as in a magic show, Ezekiel Loomis appeared from nowhere with the address and phone number of Valentine Sturgis on a piece of foolscap.

"Why I know a film actress who sings his songs!" Nigel cried. "How can I not meet him, Abner."

"He's difficult, of course, and though poorer than a whole church of mice, he's as spoiled and fussy as one of your antediluvian screen beauties. But he's still pining for a young Sicilian who stole his heart away, and then I guess the young man couldn't bear the weight of being loved and worshipped so fervently and did away with himself."

Nigel Langtree put the name and address of Val Sturgis in his breast pocket and said determinedly: "If you say so, Abner, I'll look him over."

"No, no, Nigel you must *want* to go, *want* to know him, *want* to take him up or I'll wash my hands of you forever."

"I said I'll go but you also scare me by saying how spoiled and difficult he is."

"You don't want someone malleable and tame, though, do you? You who have filmed all the retired queens of celluloid for most of your life, young man as you still are. How old are you anyway, short of forty I know."

"True, I am young," Nigel moaned. "It's my career that's old. I was only twenty-four when I directed Leatrice McEvoy in her big comeback. I nearly ended my career right then and there when I told her directly on the set she had enough makeup on to go around for all the clowns they were filming in the next studio. She bawled for an hour in her improvised tent of a dressing room – we were way out in the desert, you know. But the film was a howling success and she still wants me to direct her."

"She wanted to marry you, Nigel, if I heard correctly."

Nigel had been getting enough hints from Ezekiel Loomis to rise and depart, so now removing his untouched napkin from his collar, the film director rose, kissed Abner on his naked scalp and even threw a kiss to the impassive Ezekiel, and went off on his errand of mercy to comfort and console a fellow-sufferer, protégé of Abner Blossom, the obscure but talented Valentine Sturgis.

People wondered what on earth had been on Abner Blossom's mind when he introduced two such dissimilar parties as the world-famous film director Nigel Langtree to an obscure (at this time anyhow) composer of art songs and cantatas.

Had Abner Blossom gone mad? Kate of the Silver Screen wondered now at all of her evening soirées, and Leatrice McEvoy was even more acerbic in her condemnation of Nigel Langtree taking up with a young hillbilly from Kentucky.

But what was to astonish everybody even to greater extent was that these two dissimilar persons were to take to one another with all the fervor, the desperate need of lost souls about to sink helplessly otherwise into the night of time.

Nigel Langtree was astonished upon entering Val Sturgis's

studio to find it crammed almost to its high ceiling with every kind of ill-assorted furniture, boxes of sheet music stuffed to their brim, old china packed here and there in straw, and everywhere on wall and floor paintings and watercolors by nearly forgotten American masters of the 1930s.

"You are a collector, Mr. Sturgis," Nigel commented after shaking hands with Abner's protégé, and taking out his reading glasses he began inspecting the paintings of forgotten American masters.

Val Sturgis blushed, and tried to find a chair not covered with detritus for Nigel Langtree to sit down on.

"Ah, yes, yes," Nigel sighed as a chair was finally dragged out from the disarray around him. "You are certainly, Mr. Sturgis, in Abner Blossom's good graces. I've never heard him praise anybody living or dead as he has praised you."

Mr. Langtree kept looking about as if the disarray and confusion of the studio contradicted Mr. Blossom's evaluation of his disciple.

"May I offer you something in the way of refreshment," Val inquired nervously as he watched his guest's growing uneasiness at the confusion surrounding him everywhere.

At that very moment a picture by a once-nearly-famous painter came loose from its hanger and slipped to the floor.

Val Sturgis mumbled some brief apology.

"May I invite you instead, Mr. Sturgis, to a charming little French bistro down the street from here." Nigel gave Val one of his most ingratiating smiles usually reserved for screen stars.

"We can sit there and chat in quiet comfort and enjoy their petit dejeuner."

"Why if you would feel happier there – of course," Val tried not to reveal how offended he was by Mr. Langtree's obvious feeling of discomfort at the condition of his studio.

They proceeded then down Seventh Avenue, when all at once Nigel Langtree finally laid a hand on his new friend's shoulder and said: "Must we walk so fast, sir. I'm afraid you must be a jogger from the pace you've set for us!"

Val Sturgis stopped dead in his tracks.

"Perhaps Mr. Blossom failed to let you know I am just out

of the hospital after all." Nigel tried to soften what he saw his friend had taken for rudeness on his part.

"You're right, sir, to correct me. All my friends young or old complain about my walking so fast," Val admitted, and smiled pathetically.

They entered the fashionable bistro La Valse where the owner, a tall Frenchman who fancied he was a dead-ringer for the late General de Gaulle, gave them a cry of warm welcome, and took Nigel Langtree in his arms and cried, "Thank God, you have come back to us, monsieur."

Nigel ordered at once, almost before he had settled in his chair, but then looking at Val he realized that his friend was having some trouble making up his mind as to what he really wanted from the elaborate menu written in French.

Growing impatient at Val's indecision as to what to order, Nigel tapped loudly with his fingers on the hard wood of the table. When there was still no sign Val was ready to order, Nigel raised his voice: "Mr. Sturgis, may I be allowed to choose for you? Procrastination they say kills appetite."

Struck speechless at the curious comment, Val Sturgis dropped both his hands to his lap and surrendered to Nigel's authority.

Summoning the owner, Nigel's voice rang out through the entire restaurant:

"I will have the omelette *au naturel, café au lait,* and my friend here wishes to have the same."

"But I am on a diet, Mr. Langtree," Val spoke up now, but there was a note of submission in his voice.

"There are days, dear Mr. Sturgis, diet or no diet, when one must have something to stick to the ribs especially when one is making new friends," the film director was positive now. "Kindly trust my judgement and decision. You will see it is the best way."

Val Sturgis nodded weakly.

"Now where were we?" Nigel went on. "Ah, yes, you are of course Abner tells me writing a great number of incredible ballads and ditties."

Val stared at his new friend in gathering horror.

"Songs, Mr. Langtree, not ballads, certainly not ditties. Songs is the term today. No one writes those other things."

"Oh, well, forgive me," the film director apologized.

The owner himself now served two huge plates of omelettes.

To his annoyance, however, Nigel Langtree saw that Val was only touching his eggs with his fork and was looking distraught.

"What's amiss now?" Nigel Langtree inquired.

"I prefer my eggs a bit more done and with less butter, if it has indeed been prepared in butter."

Nigel put down his napkin on the table. The owner came forward and Nigel informed him that Mr. Sturgis was accustomed to his omelette being on the well-done side, being unacquainted with omelette *baveuse*."

The owner snatched the plate and hurried into the kitchen.

"I am afraid," Val began drinking sparingly his coffee which was too dark a roast for his taste, "I am . . ."

"What *are* you afraid of now?" the film director spoke through a mouthful of omelette, letting some of his egg fly through his teeth to the table.

"I am afraid," Val tried to phrase it inoffensively, "we may both have one thing in common, we like our own way."

Mr. Langtree laughed uproariously at this, and the owner himself brought forth the dish again with the eggs done to a different texture.

Val touched the omelette carefully with his fork, slowly lifted a bit of egg to his mouth and chewed as carefully as a patient in a dentist chair feels his new filling.

"Too dry now," Val whispered. "I'm sorry."

Nigel Langtree gestured with his napkin angrily.

"I should feel right at home with you, dear Mr. Sturgis. For you behave exactly in the same fashion as the screen stars behave when I take them out. Too dry, too moist, too brown, too underdone, too cool, too hot, too everything! My God, is it Mr. Blossom who has spoiled you so thoroughly or did you arrive from the hills in this condition!"

To Mr. Langtree's even greater astonishment and displeasure his new friend all at once burst into tears.

"Unbelievable," the film director cried as he often did when directing a particularly troublesome "take" in the studio.

A long silence followed.

"Dear Mr. Sturgis," Nigel Langtree observed. "I am afraid we are creating a scene here. Let us walk out into the soft winter air of Manhattan and forget about food for the time being. Let us go to my place on Prince Street, and there relax."

Drying his tears on his sleeve, the composer got out a choked "agreed," and the two friends rose. Mr. Langtree handed the owner an envelope, with a wink, and then followed Mr. Blossom's protégé out the door.

Nothing could have been more inauspicious than that first meeting between two men who were later to become bosom friends. Thus at any rate Abner Blossom was to summarize the meeting between Val Sturgis and the renowned Nigel Langtree of London.

Val tried to walk as slowly as Nigel Langtree as they strolled away from the French bistro.

"To my place then?" Nigel smiled encouragingly and put his arm around his new friend's shoulder.

"I'm dying to see your place," Val admitted.

"Well, we're nearly on my doorstep."

They turned abruptly down Prince Street. But Val's heart sank a little as he surveyed the dilapidated, rather ancient edifice which Nigel pointed out as the place where he lived and breathed when not in London.

They entered through a side door into a hallway which looked more like a room used for garbage disposal than the entrance to a world-famous film-maker's apartment. And when Val saw the rickety elevator they were to ride in, an elevator which rose and fell by means of what resembled a huge hangman's rope, he felt like turning tail and running fast – home. But he sighed and bit his lip.

Nigel Langtree who looked, Val observed, quite the athlete at that moment, grasped the executioner's rope in both his hands and the elevator swung jerkingly and asthmatically up and up.

Clearing his throat loudly as the lift stopped, Nigel opened the door on – yes, as Val Sturgis would later tell Abner – on glory.

It reminded Val of the time he had attended his first opera in Cincinnati. The huge opera house had been drafty, even cold. There were few people present, and those who were coughed incessantly. A rat actually ran along the aisle he was seated in. Shouts of workmen from behind the curtain reached his ears. Then all at once the enormous cerise curtain flecked with gold dust rose, and an ocean of throbbing sound broke across him, carrying him away to a world of grandeur and bliss.

A similar thing happened now when he entered Nigel Langtree's apartment. He forgot their disaffection in the bistro, forgot Nigel's nagging him for walking too fast, his fussing over the menu, forgot the hangman's rope which had hoisted them to this place of enchantment.

For everywhere he looked he saw magnificent wallpaper, imported from Paris, chandeliers which appeared to descend imperceptibly to welcome him, ancient Greek statues of fiercely naked athletes, and in the rear of the huge room to which they now made their way enlarged pictures of the great but vanished stars of the silver screen.

This array was dominated by a greatly enlarged photo of the undraped body and glistening face of a young man. That body and face in countless photos now appeared everywhere gazing down imploringly at them, in one image in particular the boy's arm reached out as if to touch the composer.

"Who in heaven's name is that?" Val almost shouted.

"You are right to say who in heaven's name," Nigel answered. "That is, that was Freddy."

"Oh, no," Val spoke softly and looked away from the photos into Nigel's eyes.

"He was my dearest, my only – " Nigel did not finish but walked out into the kitchen and called back, "What would you care to drink after our exhausting walk?"

Val could not reply for a while, lost again in the world of the photos of the dead young man who had been, he recalled from Abner's account, Nigel's only great love.

Nigel beckoned Val now to come into the kitchen which contained a dining-room table much longer and more handsome than anything Cyril Vane or Abner Blossom had ever displayed.

"This is a strong drink I have prepared for us," Nigel warned as he handed his guest a tumbler of something pale amber in color.

It was clear as the film director spoke he was trying to control his voice from breaking. Val's open admiration, his look of near-worship at the sight of the photos of the departed Franky had moved the film director to some violent turn of sorrow.

"We need it," Nigel forced a smile, and touched the drink. "And I must apologize for my ill-temper at the bistro."

Val shrugged, smiled benignly, and tasted his drink.

"What a marvelous concoction," he sipped. "And as you say, strong. It's irresistible."

Trying now to choose his words carefully, Nigel said in a low voice. "I believe you have also suffered a loss." And as he said this Nigel looked out the window at the view of several of the great skyscrapers of the metropolis and a kind of over-shadowing cathedral-like edifice close by.

"Ah, Abner spoke to you," Val said.

"Perhaps that is why Mr. Blossom insisted I get to know you, among other reasons," Nigel ventured and drank down almost all of his tall drink.

The film director walked into the recesses of the kitchen, filled his glass, looked back to see if his guest still had some, and noting Val's drink was still full, poured his old drink into a larger goblet and filled that to overflowing with something from a dusty bottle. Coming back to Val, Nigel Langtree then sat down heavily on a deeply cushioned chair.

"Because we have both lost the light of our lives, as Abner puts it, let's drink to our past happiness then, Mr. Sturgis."

They both drowsily raised their glasses and drank.

Val was becoming very uneasy for he did not want to discuss his own loss with a perfect stranger, and did not want even to mention the name of Luigi. The wound was still too excruciatingly painful, unbearable. But the drink, or perhaps the grandeur of the surroundings he found himself in, loosened his tongue. And as Val spoke of the Chimney Swift haltingly and their first meeting in the rain, Nigel Langtree also haltingly began speaking of his lost friend Freddy.

Again Val was reminded somehow of an opera. He and Nigel struck him as singers at that moment, giving out their lament over their loss, repeating time and again the well-known story, the brevity of love, the brevity of life, and the hectic sorrow and drudgery of living after love itself had gone forever never to return except in the stabs and throbs of memory.

"A match made in Heaven!" Abner Blossom greeted Ezekiel with these words as the servant was bringing in his morning repast. "Don't pout so, Zeke. It's my greatest feat of matchmaking. Oh, perhaps I missed my calling. I should have been a marriage broker. I know what you're thinking of course. Sit down, Ezekiel, like a good boy, and let me ramble on a bit."

A thin but strong smile cracked Ezekiel's usually sombre features.

In the morning light Abner saw with satisfaction that his servant's complexion had an even richer hue and a texture like that of a kind of seasoned mahogany he had observed in one of his grandmother's upstairs sea chests.

"Mr. Blossom, hear me for a second," Ezekiel began sipping his coffee topped with whipped cream and mace sprinklings. "Don't you realize or recall this is the last week of rehearsals for your opera? And we're to sit here talkin' about matchmaking?"

"Realize? Did you say *realize*?" Abner sniffed, then put a piece of brioche in his mouth and chewed in counterfeit rage. "Why can't I take my mind off the opera for an hour or so with you, my dear friend, without one of your matutinal tongue-lashings. No, no, sit, sit, don't get up to leave, I beg of you. Do not leave!"

Ezekiel kept his seat and banged his cup onto his saucer. "Where was I?"

"A match made in heaven," Zeke prompted.

"Both boys," Abner began and here Zeke gave a stifled snort for Val Sturgis would not see twenty-seven again, and the great film director Nigel Langtree must have paid farewell to forty several years ago. "Both young men," Abner began again and tapped with his solid silver spoon against the serving dish, "have had equal tragedies. In fact I thought one or both of them was going to join the choir invisible after the way they grieved. . . . But don't you see, Zeke, they can now grieve together, and a grief shared is a grief foregone.

"Listen to me, Ezekiel, let me get my mind off of that damned music drama for an hour or so – *Cock Crow!*" he repeated with anguish the opera's title. "And please, please, you don't need to make housekeeping for yourself and me such such penitence. . . ."

Raising both hands then as if he were leading his singers, Abner went on: "They met then, the two of them, Val and Nigel, and had hardly shaken hands when their quarreling and spatting began. A good omen, a meaningful presage."

Ezekiel looked down into his empty coffee cup.

"Replenish your cup, Zeke, and I'll wait till you hurry back.

"Oh, Ezekiel's nobility and grandeur! No white person can have that style!" Abner soliloquized. "It's like the force of a hurricane or tidal wave before they strike, that grandeur. And yet his magnificence is human too, though it belongs to a prince, I daresay."

Returned, Ezekiel sat again and sipped coffee and Abner went on:

"Then when poor little Val was born in a shanty in Kentucky, I take it, his mother a woman who lived in bars and was married six times, and neglected the poor lad, probably never changed his diapers. He lived on graham crackers and tea-bags until he was four when his grandmother who told fortunes and tea-leaves for a living snatched him out of the reach of his vagabond Mom. Sent him to a piano teacher and the piano teacher sent him when he finally put on his first long pants to a conservatoire in some Southern city, and lo and behold there they saw talent, maybe genius. He ran off from the South with another Kentucky chap named Hugh to arrive here with hardly enough money for a subway token. Now compare Val Sturgis's new friend and companion the spiffy, elegant, dapper almost at times grand – not as grand as you, Ezekiel, never – famed international film director, Nigel Langtree. You know how daft Americans are about Brits. All the old stars past and present, mostly past, took Mr. Langtree up and wouldn't put him down. But you know all that! He has revived, our Nigel, from the dark other shore a whole circus-load of retired lady stars, and put them back in pictures. He told me he would have given his right arm if Jeanne Eagles had been among the living, but he brought again to the light a score of other beauties from dusty oblivion. And then what happens to the little Brit, our Nigel. He falls – like our own Val Sturgis was to do later – hopelessly, smother-ingly, dementedly in love with a young racing-car driver, Freddy. As I heard it they used to stay glued together in that monstrous endlessly long flat on Prince Street. Couldn't take their eyes off one another, or their hands. Freddy was twenty-two, and yes an Antinous either naked or with his clothes on, with a hat or with his long chestnut hair trailing lazily to his shoulders. And our little Brit couldn't take a breath unless his Freddy was by his side. But more than he loved Nigel, Freddy loved racing. And Nigel followed suit. They bought one racing car after another. Were stopped I heard by hundreds of traffic policemen, arrested, often jailed, pardoned by scores of mayors and judges because of Nigel's fame and Freddy's good looks until one fog-shrouded post-meridian they rushed over the brow of a canyon out West. The car when found was hardly as recognizable as a crumpled metal can. There they lay in one another's arms, but the young driver was cold as the Nevada mountains they were near. Nigel Langtree was pulled from the wreck, given up for dead, but a smart medic thought he'd try for the impossible. Nigel all against his own will was brought back from the other shore but wanted no part of living without Freddy. But Nigel's doctor was also an Adonis! It was because of the doc's good looks and desire to retrieve the irretrievable that after a month Nigel was able to leave that midnight shore where Freddy waits for him, and slowly oh so slowly our young Brit has rejoined us. Here is where I come in, Zeke, so pay attention, I have wilfully, brazenly even introduced him to Val Sturgis. To go back to the beginning of our confab, it is a match smiled on by the gods!"

Ezekiel excused himself and went into the buttery but could hear his master going on again and again about the death of Luigi Cervo.

"Did you know, Zeke," Abner's voice reached the servant, "can you recall Luigi was called the Chimney Swift in Italian. The boy really could fly. They claim he was an acrobat for a while in Sicily. Poor Val! Still mopes, pines away, I thought myself for a while he was going to leave us too. Val Sturgis! But I pride myself here too on making him stay amongst the living. You cannot leave me now after all the work I've put into you, I scolded him, Zeke, I even shook him roughly and once slapped him. You *owe* me to live, Val Sturgis, I fulminated."

Ezekiel slowly entered the room again from the buttery very much like one of the principal tenors in *Cock Crow*. "To think you turned out to be Cupid with his bow," he said, in his deadpan way.

Abner's mouth opened wide. He was a bit shocked by Zeke's tone and his words, but then grinning as broad as a pumpkin, he laughed and said: "I expect you are, as always, right."

"Only you could have pulled it off with your matchmaking," Ezekiel said, turned and left the room.

Abner Blossom's handiwork in bringing together such dissimilar men into a strange friendship was not looked upon with
approval either by Nigel Langtree's friends or by Val Sturgis's.
The stars of the silent screen and early talkies found Val rather
on the rustic side, with his lapses in grammar and his Southern
speech – one former screen beauty dubbing him the "hillbilly,"
while Val's friends condemned Nigel as two-faced, a snob who
met Val only in secret while reserving his real alliances and
friendships for the stars of stage and films with whom he dined
and among whom he moved in majestic splendor.

But Nigel's heart had been opened by Val's own openness
and simplicity which allowed the film director to pour out his
misery and longing for the vanished Freddy. Nigel began phon-
ing Val daily, nightly, sometimes in the middle of the night.
Sometimes he telephoned him twenty times a day. Having found
the one person in all of New York who would listen to the
chronicle of his love for Freddy, Nigel soon lost all restraint like
a famished person who is at last offered his first bite of nourish-
ment.

Even Val's natural compassion and sympathy was strained
to breaking. He had never been so pursued by anyone. His time,
his privacy were no longer his own. In order to win him over
still more, Nigel loaded the young composer with favors. They
dined out regularly. He gave Val many of his cast-off but still
new custom-made shirts and neckties, or even bought him new
jackets and overcoats from the most exclusive men's shops.

Sometimes even, after a lengthy evening during which
Nigel had spoken of nothing but the nonpareil Freddy, the film
director parted from his new friend but would return in only a
few minutes to Val's building and gaze up at the lights in the
composer's flat, hungering not for love itself but for the opportunity to speak again of love, which meant to speak of Freddy.
And like a stricken lover Nigel often merely stationed himself
outside Val's building hoping against hope that Val would
emerge and allow him to tell the composer one more anecdote
taken from the life of his Freddy, show him one more snapshot
of that young god, and be allowed to weep unashamedly in the
presence of his only confidant and listener.

One evening when stationed as usual in front of Val's building Nigel saw the composer emerge, carrying something nervously in a bundle, while looking about apprehensively.

Nigel followed the composer from a safe distance. He observed that Val looked back several times, always clutching the bundle tightly against him. Block after block the chase was pursued, until to Nigel's astonishment he saw Val enter a neglected church, patronized largely by very old and devout Italian women.

On entering the church Nigel took great care to conceal himself as carefully as possible in the building's dark pillared recesses. The heavy odor of incense made him catch his breath as he knelt down keeping his head out of sight, holding a cloth over his mouth to stifle sound. Peering out from his hiding place he saw Val lighting one candle after another, and then pausing dramatically the composer began to unwrap what was in the bundle and held the object extricated up to a large statue of the Holy Virgin. Nigel saw Val's mouth move reverently as he displayed the garment he had taken out from the bundle.

Val then genuflected in front of the four or five candles he had lighted, and slowly almost agonizedly prostrated himself in front of the Cross. But a moment later he rose with sudden haste and rushed out from the church.

Nigel followed the composer for a half block or so, and then unable to restrain himself he caught up to Val and took hold of him with both his hands.

"No, for heaven's sake, no!" Val cried out, tears streaming down his face. "I ask you, please let me alone! You are persecuting me!"

"Val, listen to me," the film director began still holding his friend's hands in his. "I must speak with you. Val, I know you need help. I am your friend, can't you see that? I love you."

"Oh, Nigel, for God's sake why can't you leave me in peace. You are hounding me, spying on me, shadowing me. I can't bear it!"

Impulsively, frantically, Nigel wrenched the parcel away from Val Sturgis, who went white and made odd strangling sounds in the back of his throat.

"See here, Val. You are in no condition to be alone. You are to come to my place at once, do you hear? I won't take no for an answer. You are in too troubled a state to be by yourself." And Nigel hailed a passing cab. He pulled the composer after him into the taxi.

Arrived at the Prince Street apartment, the two men were silent for a while. After studying Val carefully Nigel walked out to the kitchen and began preparing something.

Val Sturgis began to feel a bit calmer, perhaps because of the sumptuous beauty of Nigel's living quarters, and perhaps also by reason of the film director's solicitude for him.

As the two friends drank some powerful "restorative" (Nigel's favorite term for booze), Val noted with something approaching panic that Nigel was holding tightly the bundle he had taken to the church in his hand, as if it were something vouchsafed him by the highest authority.

"What is it, Val," Nigel touched the bundle. "You must tell me. I have told you everything in my heart. Why can't you be equally open with me."

"If you open or touch it, Nigel, I will never speak to you again."

"After all we have told one another, Val. At least after all I have told you – everything that is dearest and most sacred to me I have shared. Have you any right then to be so secretive with someone who has tried to be so close to you?"

"Am I to have no privacy at all having met you? Do you treat your stars of the screen to this kind of pursuit? Let me answer for you – no, you don't, or those women would never let you see their faces again! You know it!"

"You know, Val, you are dearer to me than they are and I believe I am dearer to you than anybody you can name at this moment. Including the venerable Abner Blossom! I am asking you to open this package you have hoarded for I don't know how long and tell me why you held it up to God himself tonight in that church. Tell me, Val, you are not a Catholic, are you?"

"No, but Luigi was," Val replied desperately. "Maybe that makes me one too."

"May I open the package now, Val?"

"Open it, open it!" Val sobbed. "I see I have lost any freedom or privacy I may have ever possessed. Open it then and be done with it."

Nigel's strong fingers tore open the package. From the depths of the bundle emerged a gold-colored shirt stained here and there with red.

Val came from where he was sitting and all at once actually fell at Nigel's feet. He seized the garment from his astonished friend and held it to his face.

"But what is it, dearest Val? Tell me, please tell me."

Val's lips moved several times before he found his voice.

"When Luigi threw himself down from the building where we lived together," Val said, "he lay below for some while, crushed, almost unrecognizable. . . . While I waited beside him for the police and ambulance, I guess without knowing what I was doing, and when nobody was watching, I took off from him the gold shirt someone had once given him and I held it until my own hands were stained with the blood. When the ambulance and the police car came, I do not remember anything they said or I said until the very last moment when I remember hearing an older cop say, 'Let the poor bastard keep his friend's shirt then.'

"I think I sat there alone till nearly dawn," Val spoke after a long wait. "Only when the light came up over all the gray buildings did I really become aware of what I held in my hand, that I was holding his shirt, covered with his own blood. I would have sat on there forever perhaps until I don't know who it was came by, maybe more police, maybe Good Samaritans, maybe angels themselves, and they helped me back to my flat."

"No, it can't be!" Abner Blossom cried as he rode in a limousine with the conductor of the orchestra for his opera, Adam Cantrell.

"What is it, maestro?" the conductor wondered and stared

out the window of the car at the man Abner was pointing out with such amazement.

"It's Nigel Langtree, Adam, if my eyes don't deceive me! Coming out from Our Lady of Pompeii church! And look, he is wiping his eyes like one of the faithful! I can't believe he is a communicant. Adam, do you mind, let's give him a lift."

The limousine came to a halt, and at the sound of the car's brakes, Nigel Langtree looked about nonplussed as he heard his name called both by the composer of *Cock Crow* and by the conductor of the opera.

"Get in, get in," Abner commanded irritably. "Sit up there with the driver, why don't you, we have the back seat here covered with music scores."

Nigel gave out a huge sigh, and daubed at his eyes.

"Are you a practising RC now, my dear boy?" Abner raised his voice as the car sped away.

"Ah, I may become one, Abner," Nigel responded and he began shaking hands now at an introduction to Adam Cantrell.

"But we know one another, Abner," Nigel finally managed to overcome his surprise. "We've been friends for decades – Adam and I!

"How are the rehearsals going?" Nigel forced out the words.

"Should we tell him, Adam," Abner turned to the conductor.

"Don't let Abner run down his own show," Adam Cantrell said. "Things are going wonderfully."

"The leading soprano has quit," Abner pointed out. "And the tenor is only interested in the boys in the chorus, and won't memorize his words, just giggles and chokes over what he can't remember. But he is a young Adonis and has a voice that could reach Coney Island with no trouble. But my conductor here is all the gods could bestow on me."

"Abner, if you'll be so kind," the conductor spoke in the composer's good ear. "This is my stop, dear maestro."

"You won't come back with Nigel and me for a nightcap."

"I must beg off, maestro. Please forgive me. And so good to run into you again, Nigel."

"Ah, well," Abner said as the car drew up to the curb. "See you tomorrow, Adam, dear fellow, at the salt mines, and an avalanche of thanks to you for all you are, and all you do." And Abner bestowed a fervid kiss on the conductor's rubicund face as he was helping himself out of the car.

"And now, Nigel, to my digs. For I've got to know what has set you snivelling and drying your eyes on Irish handkerchiefs in an Italian Catholic church."

Nigel, too weak to protest, was driven away by Abner without one more word of protest.

As Abner was preparing the film director one of his special nightcaps, a free version of *café au diable*, with the usual assortment of tiny sandwiches, Nigel made a brave attempt to stop sobbing. Of course the old composer overheard it, and handing Nigel his drink, scowled and said: "Tell Papa everything."

"But my dear friend, you already know everything of what's going on inside me. And where on earth is Ezekiel?"

"Ezekiel doesn't spend the night here, Nigel. Though I would be a happier man if he did. No, no, Ezekiel has a family. Has a grown son of twenty-one, and claims he wants to begin breaking him in as my manservant."

Nigel brightened and sipped at his drink.

"I would have sworn Ezekiel was never old enough to have a son of that age," Nigel began to relax a bit. "Africans somehow always look younger than we washed-out white folks."

"Being a Brit, Nigel, you don't know African Americans very well, do you. Ezekiel always has lied about his age, as he has every right to do. And let me tell you, it came as a shock to me also that he had a grown son of twenty-one. He kept that a secret until just the other day."

Abner wet his lips with his drink and sat thoughtful.

"Ezekiel always gives me the impression he knows everything about everybody," Nigel spoke perhaps too softly for Abner to hear.

"And now, Nigel, let me in to your secret. What were you doing in that neighborhood and in that temple of idolators."

"You sound like my dear departed mother, Abner," Nigel protested. "I don't know what she would think looking down from her Methodist heaven at her son lighting candles in a Roman temple for my dear Franky and genuflecting. It's all your fault anyhow, Abner."

Abner smiled contentedly.

"For introducing me to your Val Sturgis. Seems, Abner, Val still keeps the gold shirt his Luigi died in, and I surprised him the other day as he entered Our Lady of Pompeii with that shirt which he proceeded to show to the Divine Mother after lighting four or five candles."

"I envy both of you for letting your feelings carry you away. I belong to quite a different generation, you've got to remember. Where the head is always right and the heart never. But if that is how you both feel, why shouldn't you act on those feelings even if it carries you to idolatry."

Nigel was struck by Abner's cold air of reason. He saw that more than generations separated him and Val from the old composer. They belonged to different worlds.

"But I want to hear about your opera, Abner. The papers carry almost nothing else but news about it. And I've had enough of my own heartache and sorrow."

"I am being blackmailed," Abner began, "or perhaps something worse by Olga Petrovna." Abner lowered his voice in confidence as if the widow of Cyril Vane might perhaps be eavesdropping on them somewhere in the hall.

"She, that is Olga, has called here innumerable times, has hired a score of lawyers and detectives – now that she's rich as Croeus, she wants my opera stopped on the grounds she is a character in it, and her husband is defamed by my portrayal of his character. . . . But, Nigel, my backers and the show's management are solidly behind me. The show will go on." Abner rose and refilled their cups.

"The saddest news of the week is that dear Harlan Yost who waited on Cyril Vane hand and foot for twenty years – you remember Harlan of course. Well, Harlan was not remembered in Cyril Vane's will except for an old camera and some darkroom equipment which Olga was going to throw out in any case. The rumor of course has it that Olga Petrovna and her lawyers changed the will on the grounds Cyril was *non compos mentis* at the time he had his will drawn up. Shouldn't the law now decree, though, that Olga Petrovna is herself certifiably a lunatic?"

Nigel laughed, even purred now with delight.

"How I envy you, Abner," Nigel confided. "You are so poised, so in control, never at a loss for a word or knowledge of what is going on. You are so yourself. While chaps like Val Sturgis and me are fair game to our own feelings."

"Oh, twaddle, and you know it. I've been hit by Cupid's bow too, but that was before you were born."

Nigel beamed and nodded, and let Abner pour him more drink.

"I can't wait till *Cock Crow* opens in that marvelously wonderful-horrible amphitheater in Brooklyn," Nigel showed genuine enthusiasm.

"God only knows what will be its fate," Abner reflected. "But the world is still talking about *The Kinkajou*, so let us hope destiny will be kind to my new offspring. But we'll all live through it even if it founders to the bottom of the East River."

Nigel rose now and took the composer in his arms.

"Talk about nonpareil, Abner, you've got it all, you're everything I wish I could create in films. And here am I – discovered clandestinely by America's greatest opera composer, sneaking out of Our Lady of Pompeii where I paid my respects to my vanished Franky by lighting candles and going down on my knees."

Abner Blossom often liked to recall, and even more now, that he had after all been a soldier, a second lieutenant in the war his generation had called the Great War. And now as another dread day approached, the day of his opera's première, the work of his old age, he felt the necessity for all of soldiering he could muster. He had not really slept for a week, thinking of the first night of

Cock Crow. He finally could do nothing but pace and shudder. What had he written at this late hour of his life? Was the opera as great, even as shocking as his friends and the young conductor and the singers claimed, or was it after all only some concocted confection such as wealthy women bought at Rumpelkammer's to solace their lonely and fading sorrows.

Alarmed by his master's worry, even dread, Ezekiel did something which he realized was taking a long chance, something as daring perhaps as composing an opera in an uncivilized and tasteless age.

Unannounced, Ezekiel brought his 21-year-old son Malachi to be with Abner at this time of crisis.

"Yes, to watch over you," Ezekiel had raised his voice as he came into Abner's work room, pushing ahead of him his only-begotten son.

Then Zeke saw the look of pleasure, gratitude, relief on Abner's face. It was not dissimilar to the look a mother often gives when the doctor holds up for her her own new-born.

"What a gift from providence," Abner quoted from one of his own operatic arias.

"Malachi will stay every night if you so wish, and of course he'll be here during the day. Malachi is dependable, able, sterling."

Ezekiel then paused like an actor who waits for his cue to go on. But Abner Blossom only beamed gratitude in response.

"Meanwhile," Ezekiel scolded, "I see you've left lots of work in the kitchen and buttery!"

At Abner's bidding Malachi sat down in the large chair facing the composer. He was even darker, if that was possible, than his father, but his crisp tightly ringletted hair was almost blond. His lips were more gracefully formed than Ezekiel's and he wore at least four rings on his hands and a nearly invisible earring in his right ear lobe. He looked confidently and calmly and warmly into Abner's eyes.

"There's crowds everywhere outside," Malachi found his voice. "And all over the Brooklyn Bridge."

"Crowds?" Abner wondered. He felt calmer, almost his old self indeed now that the son had been brought in by his father.

"Yes, sir, they're coming in droves for the opera tonight," Ezekiel Loomis's stentorian voice broke in as he carried in a tray of snacks.

It was a daring feat, and Abner loved daring – the serving of his son Malachi along with the master.

Abner bowed as he often did at the conclusion of one of his own song recitals. "To think I've got both of you today," he chuckled. "And here all these years, Zeke, you've kept hidden from me you were married and had offspring, and above all, that you had Malachi! Yes, you're a master of surprises, not to mention secrets. Your Dad should have been made a magician!" He spoke this last to Malachi.

"But where's your cup, Zeke," Abner scolded when he saw only he and Malachi were being served.

"No time for that," Ezekiel complained. "You should see the kitchen. Oh the mess out there!"

"Yes, I've had visitors galore. Nigel Langtree stayed till four this morning weeping like Niobe, groaning like Demeter. Did you ever mourn for a lost love like that," Abner inquired of Zeke. "And went down on your knees in front of lighted candles to the departed one? I bet you never did."

Ezekiel exchanged a worried look with Malachi and vanished.

"And now, Malachi," Abner announced, "I must look over my score once again." And to his pleased satisfaction, Abner saw Malachi following him into his work room.

"Can you read music, Malachi?" Abner asked.

"Oh, yes," Ezekiel's son answered.

"And can you sing as you read?"

Malachi nodded.

"Begin here," Abner pointed to a part of the opera score he was still not satisfied with.

Without so much as clearing his throat, Malachi Loomis held the score firmly in his hand and commenced to sing.

"What a lovely resonant baritone! Fills the entire room."

But as Malachi sang, Abner, in one of his most characteristic ways, had nodded, had begun to doze, and then not having had sleep for so long, lulled by Malachi's voice, fell for a while fast asleep in his chair.

Meanwhile, without the scandal of *The Kinkajou* having died down, the anticipation of seeing the even more controversial opera *Cock Crow* had stirred both the black and the white citizens of Manhattan and especially Brooklyn. Crowds were continuously streaming across the Brooklyn Bridge to try to secure at least standing room for an event which had aroused general interest.

The mayor had called out as many emergency squads of police and plainclothesmen as possible. City Hall feared a riot as much as Abner feared the failure of his musical masterpiece.

The entire city was breathless. As the haggard afternoon of the première drew on, Abner's closest friends gathered round him. He was persuaded to take some real sustenance and place less reliance on his concoctions of brandy, rum, hot black coffee and cloves.

Everybody around him saw Abner was near panic.

Then just a few minutes before the hired limousine was to arrive for the composer and his entourage, Abner's eye was caught by a framed photograph of himself and Cyril Vane together near the Eiffel Tower, in Paris, in the 1920s. All at once he felt reassured, blessed, peaceful, ready. Approaching the photograph he spoke aloud: "I tried to do you justice, my friend. But one can't make an omelette, can one, without the breaking of eggs. I have portrayed you as I saw you, dear Cyril, glorious, dreadful, impossible, wonderful, scintillating, maddeningly wicked and angelic by turns, living as you saw fit without any attempt to be someone you could never have been anyhow. You were never anybody but you!" To the pleased astonishment of Nigel Langtree, Val Sturgis, and several other young admirers, he kissed the photo. Close to them stood an immaculate and dignified Harlan Yost who must have heard Abner's soliloquy to his departed employer.

Turning to all his friends, Abner cried:

"But they say, be advised, *she* will turn up tonight if not with firearms, at least firecrackers. *She* has warned everyone that she means to bring ruin to me and my opera. I speak of course of Olga Petrovna. She says she will stop the show if it kills her on the spot. My informant is her one-time Russian paramour, Count Alexander Ilitch whom, gentlemen, I have finally won over. We have entered into an *entente cordiale*."

And with that speech they were all leaving Abner Blossom's apartment when footsteps were heard from the back regions of the suite, and Malachi ran up to Abner, breathless.

"Am I not, sir, to be in your company?"

Abner embraced him and everyone hurried down to the front hotel exit.

As Abner stood near the hotel exit surrounded by his closest friends, two plainclothesmen approached the composer and asked for a word with him. Drawing Malachi along, Abner followed the police into an empty studio down the hall.

When Abner and Malachi returned after the conference to face the worried countenances of the composer's friends, Abner raised both his arms:

"It's all right, gentlemen," Abner spoke out, but he looked peaked and drawn and held on to Malachi as he spoke. "There has been a bomb threat, but the performance will go on!"

Everyone cheered. The atmosphere, Abner felt, was beginning to resemble that before a high-school football match. But then Abner himself was almost as American as high-school football, under a thin varnish of Parisian chic.

There was an unnerving calm outside on the street which recalled to the old composer his memories of the Great War when he had been stationed near Paris. He would not have been surprised now if he had heard once again the rumble of artillery, the thunder of cannon. He smiled as he recalled Paris, and then coming back to the present he recognized Malachi who had all at once become part and parcel of his entourage as if he had always lived with Abner at the Hotel Enrique and had no intention of ever leaving.

Ezekiel, standing as always aloof from everyone else, was listening carefully to his tiny transistor radio. At a scowl from Abner he shut the radio off and took his place with the other guests.

But what Ezekiel had heard on his transistor made him realize he was no longer in charge at the buttery and parlor, but was a spectator at a public event. For the announcer described in detail how thousands of curiosity-seekers as well as ticket-holders were crossing the Brooklyn Bridge. Traffic was at an all-time impasse. The African community, the radio voice had gone on, was divided in its feelings concerning *Cock Crow*. Some felt this idyll of a white man's love and admiration for the black race was demeaning to the New African, while others of the black population saw it as the first time an opera had extolled without false shame or condescension the dynamism and charm, beauty and inextinguishable vigor of African America.

The limousine now drove up. Abner sighed, was helped into his greatcoat by Ezekiel, rejected a walking stick, and settled his top hat on his head at a severe angle.

Val Sturgis and Nigel Langtree, now inseparable, piled in the car close to Abner and Malachi.

There was still a sizeable crowd outside the Enrique as they were departing. But large as it was, it was neither as boisterous nor as loud as some of the crowds had been earlier in the day. This crowd gave out a kind of low murmur of tempered applause and admiration as the limousine began to move. Several older blacks raised their hats and called out the composer's name.

"We have done all that can be done," Abner spoke a few last words as he waved to the crowd. "Now everything is in the lap of the gods."

The cheering rose in volume as Abner and his retinue were swept away in the enormous car, and a bravura shriek of new tires drowned out the last of the huzzas, and then all that could be seen was the enormous red tail light of the vehicle, eloquent in the fading daylight.

The limousine came to an abrupt stop at the entrance to the Brooklyn Bridge. All of the occupants continued talking for a while, but slowly the conversation and laughter ceased.

Abner prodded the partition between him and the driver. Abner raised his voice and demanded to know the cause of the delay. A few angry words followed, and the driver banged shut the partition.

"Our man suggests that we get out and walk," Abner explained to his guests. "Seems the entire bridge is jammed up for miles and miles and nothing is moving."

When a stony silence fell upon Abner's fellow-passengers, Abner raised his voice in his most military manner: "He has advised us, our kind chauffeur, and I expect he is after all right, that if we hope to get to the Amphitheater tonight we had best follow his advice and walk."

This intelligence struck everyone dumb. It was Abner who, without further ado, got out of the limousine first, and pointed gleefully to the walk waiting for them ahead.

"It will do us all a world of good," the composer exorted his friends, and he set off toward the sidewalk at a fast clip.

"Ah, look around you," he shouted, "do you see all the lights, the wonder of the metropolis's back door! Those lights look like so many glasses filled with red and orange jelly, don't you think?"

All of Abner's assemblage now began walking in the direction of the Amphitheater, all were worried whether the composer would be able to make it. But they had forgotten Abner's boast of his pedigree, the iron constitution of his ancestors, his mother, grandmother, great-grandmother all having lived beyond the century mark.

"Ah well," he told them, panting a little, "yes maybe I feel a little bushed, but with Malachi here to look after me, can I complain?"

Abner's friends began to relax a little when they saw he was not winded by the walk and was indeed taking great pleasure in observing the sights and sounds of the harbor. Many of the other persons walking on the pedestrian bridge recognized Abner Blossom and shouted to him that they were coming to his world première.

All at once they ran into squad after squad of policemen. There was again whispered talk of a riot, a bomb threat and a knot of protestors shrieked out that the opera *Cock Crow* had vicious racial overtones, down-grading the entire African race, and was indecent into the bargain, sullying as it did the great Cyril Vane and his Russian-born wife, Olga Petrovna.

Grateful in a way that his deafness obliterated many of his antagonists' strictures, the composer stopped every few feet to greet his admirers, who outnumbered the detractors, and he would wave his hands and then, reeling a bit from all the exertion, he would rest his hand on the broad shoulders of Malachi, who would look down almost worshipingly at his father's employer and long-time friend.

At long last they reached the entrance to the Amphitheater. Abner and his friends gasped at the sight of the beautiful vulgarity and tackiness of the marquee with enormous revolving rose lights spelling out his name and

THE FINAL APOTHEOSIS OF OPERA
COCK CROW
THE WORLD WILL NEVER BE THE SAME,
NOR WILL YOU: WORLD PREMIERE TONITE

A crowd of admirers now blotted out a smaller faction of opponents, and the supporters gathered protectively round Abner and his retinue. A veritable Hallelujah Chorus lifted their powerful voices in tribute to the man who had brought Africa such renown and splendor in music.

"Abner is in his glory," Val Sturgis whispered in Nigel Langtree's ear. "How he adores being adored!"

Nigel smiled. He wanted to say he would give anything in the world if Freddy could be with them, then bit his lip to keep his emotion under control.

The atmosphere was exceptionally electric, spiced with a hint of danger, alluring and fraught with mystery.

Nearly everyone was black and nearly everyone was youthful. Even the middle-aged and old appeared to be gaining in strength and vigor, grace and poise. Unlike the audiences at other opera houses all the spectators who were moving into the Amphitheater could easily be mistaken for members of the cast of the opera itself.

It was a crowd which had come to witness perhaps a

miracle, and from a miracle they hoped to be carried beyond mere entertainment to rapture, ecstasy, delirium.

An uneasy hush fell on all who were already seated when Abner and his cohorts entered. Then belated cheers broke out, cries of encouragement and bravos as at a bull fight or some star-studded boxing match.

The neighing of horses was audible from behind the enormous scarlet curtain and one heard the crack of a whip and shouts in a foreign language.

As Abner seated himself in the midst of his friends, the orchestra began assembling, and the discordant notes of instruments tuning up were heard and an argument from the performers in the string section.

From the balconies floated down crimson balloons and shiny ribbons and sequined festoons bearing words of greeting.

Abner pressed the arm of Malachi tightly, then when the applause grew in volume he rose stiffly, assisted by the youth, and bowed as deeply as he was able in the Grand Opera manner – perhaps more in the tradition of the great Barnum.

Ezekiel, on the other side of Abner, now watched him closely. One of the burdens Abner inflicted upon his friends was his tendency to fall fast asleep, especially at ceremonies in his honor. To avert this, Ezekiel had given Malachi a bottle marked *Restorative* which the younger Loomis was to administer if the composer started to doze. A gold-plated spoon was attached to the bottle.

But then an event transpired which made a restorative unnecessary. Abner, to his trepidation, even horror, caught sight of someone looking down fixedly on him from the most lavishly furnished box overlooking the stage: Olga Petrovna herself. She raised her jewel-studded lorgnette and gave the composer an enigmatic look followed by faint derisive smiles, and finally a stiff bow. Olga wore a hat crowned with lilies, a hat not seen in public since the end of the last century. Her thin, even emaciated throat was embraced by a heavy diamond choker.

"Doom is looking down upon us," Abner breathed to Ezekiel. Malachi at that moment drew out the bottle of restorative, but Ezekiel gave his son a severe look of command to put the bottle away.

Finally both the late-comers and the uninvited began moving into the aisles of the Amphitheater. There was an air of taut expectancy everywhere, as if some long-absent exalted personage might finally step on to the stage and initiate the evening's gala. Then the house lights flickered and went down, there was a spasm of coughing and last-minute exchanges of confidences, and the lavish overture drowned out all other sounds.

Eloi Bordelon, the noted bass baritone taking the part of Cyril Vane, appeared from nowhere as if dropped from a balloon. Those who knew Cyril Vane's photographs of Eloi gasped for this was the first time they had seen the African star when he was not unclothed and covered with sequins and wrestling oil.

But Eloi's voice rose above his earlier renown, and the audience knew this was a voice without peer as he began to sing the aria which was to become world famous:

Love has no boundary,
nor bliss any summit

Abner kept shaking his head, but then finally he began to smile, even grin, and let his head fall almost to his hands in gratitude when uncontrollable applause blotted out the last notes of the bass baritone's rendering.

Then slowly, ambiguously, mysteriously, began the story of the secret life of Cyril Vane and of his worship of the Negro race, incarnated in singers, trapeze artists, dancers, and athletes.

No sooner had Eloi Bordelon, as Cyril Vane, started singing than the soprano Agatha Loveguard entered, wearing a gown of such outlandish extravagance the audience was at first unable to appreciate they were hearing one of the great voices of the last fifty years.

Agatha Loveguard, as Olga Petrovna now sang the aria:

I forsook my native land
to be bond-slave to Love

in bitter-sweet tones.

The audience demanded that La Loveguard repeat the aria twice, and at its second rendition Abner Blossom rose and bowed again and again and finally waved to the two balconies above him.

By the end of the first act it was overwhelmingly obvious that the opera was a resounding smash-hit.

As the scent of furs, and expensive perfumes accompanied by the undeniable tang of sweat circulated through the vast auditorium, Abner tugged at Malachi's sleeve, requesting a sip of the restorative. Malachi produced the gold-plated spoon and measured out the required number of drops, which Abner drank carefully.

People passing by the composer's party could not refrain from loudly congratulating him. At the same time a mood of apprehension was beginning to manifest itself. At the height of all this preoccupation, Abner saw with relief Val Sturgis approaching, bearing a glass of foamy Danish beer.

"God knows, my dear Val, what I have swallowed in this restorative." Val held Abner's hand briefly in a strong grip.

Then looking up, Abner saw that the box occupied by Olga Petrovna was empty. Only her ermine stole rested on the ornate chair she had recently sat in. But one white, not over-clean glove, hung over the gleaming edge of the box.

Turning to Val, Abner observed, "Perhaps, my friend, I should have conducted after all, don't you see."

During the lengthy intermission, a man of severe and ruggedly overbearing appearance speaking with another man of equally severe mien kept looking in the direction of Abner Blossom and his friends. The more impressive and older of the two men now advanced over to Val Sturgis, and bent down whispering through strong liquorish breath: "May I have a private word with you, sir?"

As Val rose he saw to his relief that Abner was entirely engrossed now in reading the program notes. Val had an almost demented fear of the police, and he knew it was a plainclothesman who had asked him to follow him outside.

"You're Mr. Sturgis, the composer, I believe," the officer began. "I don't want to frighten you or your friends, certainly not Mr. Blossom, but we have had four bomb threats this evening. All have been immediately investigated and found to be without verification. But," and here the officer took hold of Val's right arm with painful pressure, "you will notice that we have placed Mr. Blossom and company very near the big fire door. Should there be any disturbance, will you please usher the composer out immediately."

The police officer then saluted Val smartly and, speaking now in his normal voice, said, "Good evening, sir."

Val was not reassured by the plainclothesman's report, and his arm ached from the man's vice-like pressure. On returning to his seat he saw with amusement that Abner was being helped again to the bottle of restorative by Malachi Loomis. He recalled now that in the room Abner called his Buttery, there was a veritable pharmacopoeia of bottles containing tinctures and herbals for every complaint which afflicts body and soul. Val would have given a lot at that moment to know what the bottle of restorative contained. At least it was keeping Abner awake.

The second act of the opera was as brilliant as the first. Val had never thought that Abner Blossom could have written such strongly melodic yet moving arias as those that now issued from the throats of the very singers whom had been at his beck and call since they were hardly more than children. There were at least three generations of black singers performing that night, and as Val reflected, all of them had also been in constant attendance before the camera of Cyril Vane.

A kind of general intoxication was spreading over the audience. The air was filled with a palpitating energy made more intense by the fact that those who had not been able to obtain seats were now moving forward from their standing position so that the entire auditorium gave the impression it was rising, moving, even levitating, one might say, and this sensation brought back to Val Sturgis the memory of Luigi and his rising up before his eyes. Looking at his side he saw that Nigel Langtree was also moved to a kind of incoherent delirium of pleasure.

The trombones took over, followed by seven young male alto voices. Val had never suspected anyone outside of the most exalted jazz masters could have written such music. The audience demanded encore after encore from the trombonists and the male altos.

The second act, which detailed Cyril Vane's forays into Harlem and its secret sanctuaries of abandon, ended with a general frenzy both on the part of the singers and the audience. The spectators might have continued to applaud had not a second, brand-new curtain descended, in front of which stood the singer Clarissa Turpin who urged them to leave their seats and seek the fresh air.

Val watched Abner worriedly during the intermission. The excitement and the joy shown by the audience was beginning to have their effect on the composer. Dark circles were forming under his eyes, and his jaw trembled.

Then Val saw with some relief that Ezekiel was brandishing another bottle from the Abner's private pharmacopoeia. At first the composer declined, but when Ezekiel imperiously insisted, Abner reached out his hand and drank thoughtfully from the bottle itself, and then handed it back to his servant who measured carefully how much had been imbibed.

"And one of these, please, sir," Ezekiel handed Abner a scarlet pastille which the old composer took obediently and began to eat.

"There are crowned heads here tonight," Abner spoke in his old sour all-knowing voice. "Did you catch a glimpse of Baroness Komeni?" he inquired. "She has not appeared in public for twenty years, but she swore to me on the phone she would come tonight if it was her last appearance on earth. Look at her waving to us, Val." Abner rose and bowed low to a woman in a box overlooking their seats. She was holding an ostrich-plume fan, the very one Cyril Vane had photographed her holding tightly in her beringed hand so many decades before.

"It is both hot and cold in the amphitheater," Abner remarked as the orchestra began making its noisy reappearance, and the house lights were again flickering and beginning to dim.

"I rather like the two kinds of temperature," Abner rambled on. "Reminds one of school days when we would eat a hot fudge sundae and the hot sauce of the chocolate contrasted with the icy quality of the ice cream."

"Your opera is like a hot fudge sundae, Abner," Nigel Langtree spoke rather daringly. Everyone held his breath at such a remark, but Abner showed he agreed and chuckled.

There was perhaps only one reason why Abner Blossom did not doze in his seat on the night of the première of his opera. He had after all been dozing after dinner for at least twenty years, and all the cries of bass trombones and soprano saxophones would not have prevented his taking a cat-nap. No, none of that. He dared not doze because of the presence of Olga Petrovna. He watched the box above and marked how she flitted in and out, always leaving behind on her absences her ermine stole and fan as a reminder to him, he felt, that she was not far away, and would reappear.

Abner dared not even mention the fact she was present to his friends. He felt that to name the woman would give power to her to work mischief, and mischief he was sure she would perpetrate tonight, no matter how loud the great voices of the bass baritone and dramatic sopranos soared forth, no matter how sweetly the chorus of male altos enchanted the thronging audience.

Olga was waiting, Abner knew, and his skin actually crawled at the thought – she was waiting for her cue in the opera (for she had got hold of the libretto through trickery), her cue which would be when the character of Cyril Vane refuses to enter Paradise unless it be into the Colored section of Heaven.

The producer, the director and the publicity manager had all balked a bit at this off-key denouement of the opera, but at last Abner Blossom's international reputation had persuaded them to let the end of the opera stand as it was written.

Although Cyril Vane and Olga Petrovna were the only persons of the white race in the opera itself, Abner had insisted that a renowned black singer should undertake the role of the photographer and litterateur. Eloi Bordelon had accepted the role of Cyril, and his swooningly beautiful voice and still-manly figure won all hearts at the opera's première.

During the third act Abner consumed almost an entire bottle of restorative, but to his undying gratitude, Ezekiel suddenly produced a substitute, even larger with the words *eau-de-vie* in shining cerise and gold letters.

Cyril Vane's death scene was perhaps the most successful moment of the opera, even if not the most telling musically.

"I haven't Puccini's gift for tears and pathos," Abner Blossom later told a knot of reporters. "And Cyril Vane never knew true sorrow, not rock-bottom sorrow at any rate, and like his life his death was painless."

At last engulfed by the sweet smell of success, jolted ceaselessly by the oceanic cascade of applause and "bravos" Abner, despite the support of the new bottle of *eau-de-vie*, suddenly felt the icy hand of true terror. He felt more aware than at any time in his life, certainly since the time when as a boy he had fallen from his grandfather's buggy into the icy water of the upper Mississippi, and come close to dying of exposure.

For looking up he saw – who else? Olga Petrovna entering the opera stage from the wings. She carried something under her opera cloak which, gradually loosening, fell to the floor. She held in her hand a pearl-handled pistol, and pointed it skywards.

Then lowering the gun – she leveled it at – who else – Abner Blossom though he was too far away to be reached by her bullets.

But then perhaps carried away by her own memories of stardom, she began in a voice which still carried, to sing of her long years of torment and martyrdom – and she used the word "crucifixion" once – singing while now pointing to the black singer impersonating her husband, whose aria at this moment required him to sue Saint Peter for permission to enter the Colored section of Paradise.

Strangely enough, the audience almost unanimously thought the entrance of Madame Petrovna was part of the opera, and though her voice was peculiarly ragged, it had an abrupt, wild and discordant something which made it pass for the real thing; except that the young conductor, Adam Cantrell, unnerved by her appearance, dropped his baton, and the rest of the orchestra went off into jazzy improvisation and soaring *fortissimo* abandon.

But suddenly Olga was raising the gun.

She fired once.

Cries came from throats of some of those seated in the first row, but those cries were also taken by the audience as part and parcel of the opera.

Eloi Bordelon, bass baritone, then stepped forward, and though later everyone realized he had been grazed by one of Olga's bullets, he seized Olga Petrovna, the screen star of 1915, and having been an athlete in his young days, carried her above his head into the wings to applause which caused some of the plaster of the ancient Amphitheater, older even than Olga Petrovna, to drift down on to the stage and first rows, like the season's first snowflakes.

Abner Blossom sank back in his seat after this extravagant outrage. Abner's friends feared he was close to a fainting fit. A thin ribbon of red fluid soiled his French collar, but there was a look on his face – one could not quite call it happiness, but perhaps ecstasy. His head turned, to fall into the amarinthine curls of Malachi Loomis.

What brought back Abner from the Other Shore was his gradual perception that the audience had been completely taken in by Olga Petrovna's unscheduled appearance as the neglected wife of Cyril Vane. Indeed the audience was still applauding Madame Olga's appearance out of the blue. The entire auditorium had risen now as if one, applauding Abner, the opera, the orchestra, the trombone soloists, the young male altos, but where oh where was the unknown prima donna who had won their admiration, even breathless awe – she with the pearl-handled revolver and great opera cloak?

It was only then that Abner realized that the entire audience had been wholly taken in, duped, by the Russian emigrée who had quarreled with Cyril Vane for nearly fifty years, and had eaten her heart out at being relegated to the wings in Cyril Vane's own opera house on Central Park West. Tonight, however briefly, Olga Petrovna had starred!

"The audience believed it, Malachi!" Abner confided to

Ezekiel Loomis' son.

Later Abner described the spectators as parting like the Red Sea to make way for him and his guests as they left by courtesy of the police force through a special exit.

It was early spring and the air was cold. The coolness was just what Abner Blossom required. He was coming out of his terror.

Olga Petrovna had, instead of stopping the show, made it a hit, and restored "Grand" to "Opera." And not a soul in the sea of spectators suspicioned she was not in or of it!

"May I offer you a cigarette, dear Mr. Blossom?" A young man in evening dress approached the composer, extending the box of imported cigarettes Abner had not laid eyes on since his great days in the City of Light.

"I will tonight," Abner thanked the unknown young man. He accepted the gold-tipped cigarette as the donor lit it for him and watched devoutly as Mr. Blossom inhaled his first mouthful of smoke.

Ezekiel stared woodenly at his employer for he had never seen Abner smoke, and had indeed been lectured time and again on the habit until Ezekiel had finally renounced tobacco entirely.

"Ah, well," Ezekiel addressed his son Malachi. "Why not, then, tonight?"

At that moment in this long intermission before the final act, a loud explosion froze every one standing outside the opera house. But a policeman walked hurriedly over to the Abner Blossom group and whispered to Abner: "It's quite all right, sir. They're having a joke down the street with firecrackers."

"Are we then all prepared for the final act, my children?" Abner wondered, throwing down the elegant French cigarette from which he had taken only two or three puffs, and was still coughing from his enjoyment of those.

"Where do you suppose they have taken Madame Petrovna?" Val Sturgis managed to ask Nigel Langtree. But Nigel had fallen into one of his brooding spells, and only shrugged his shoulder.

The audience was restless, for it was feared the final act could not equal the intensity, abandon, and manic climax of the third act. Their apprehensions were unfounded, as a grudging press would later admit, for the final act cast in the shade all previous three acts of the opera.

No one, it was later claimed, had ever written music for the soprano sax, the trombone, the oboe and the horn as Abner Blossom had composed for those instruments in the swan song of his long career.

And then – that other instrument, the human voice. Who had dared write such music for the young male alto, but Abner! And the chorus of unrestrained Africans, whose lungs were themselves trumpets, outdoing at times the brass.

Or what of the chorus of bugles or the three player pianos?

Had the audience all been smoking not French cigarettes but cocaine, their intoxication during the final act could not have been more complete. As the last act approached its climax the audience began, unbidden, moving toward the stage itself. Some even walked up on to the stage and merged with the singers.

The old Amphitheater appeared to be both expanding and contracting with the unprecedented unstinted all-consuming Niagara of sound. Everything trembled as though in the aftershock of an earthquake.

When the very last curtain call came, the audience turned (and certainly Ezekiel if not Malachi was terror-stricken) toward the composer of this unheard-of musical extravaganza.

The crowd surrounded Abner so closely that a stalwart young man (who might have stepped out of the photographic studio of Cyril Vane himself) hoisted the half-conscious composer on his shoulders by way of protection. A gathering of young black men wearing tuxedos and top hats acted as reinforcements to secure Abner's safety.

"To the bridge, the bridge then!" some voices urged.

Abner's own friends followed worriedly but gradually fell in with the exuberance of the hour and were shouting words which they themselves probably did not understand.

All eyes turned to Abner being borne away on the shoulders of his dusky admirer. As this strange procession bearing the composer made its way toward the Brooklyn Bridge, it seemed to every eye they were viewing a final coda to the opera itself, and to make this impression more credible, a group of trombone and horn players brought up the rear playing in jazzy cacophony.

All at once from out of the dark a limousine a good thirty feet long slid up to the procession of revellers and athletes. Two men in full evening dress leapt from the car, and shouted commands in English and Spanish. The young bearer of Abner obeyed their shouts, and allowed the composer to alight from his shoulders.

Abner blinked at one last detail from the spectacle surrounding him: it was the presence of – yes – torch lights. Everywhere he could look there were blazing, leaping, gushing torch lights held by black, brown, even pale hands.

The opera had flowered into life and was coming to an end in the Brooklyn night with thousands of new spectators. The life of Cyril Vane had been further expanded into this uncouth but eloquent tribute from untutored throats and lungs.

The management of the Hotel Enrique where Abner Blossom had resided for over forty years stirred uneasily by reason of the massive acclaim being visited upon their tenant and upon the hotel itself. (Abner had further embarrassed the hotel by constantly referring to himself as their "star boarder.")

"Success," said the manager in one of the hotel's daily business meetings, "success, gentlemen, can be as calamitous as failure, perhaps more so."

The manager's comment was conveyed to Abner (who remained now in bed most of the time), and the remark brought forth a chuckle from the composer.

"Ezekiel, I have some news to share with you," Abner said one gloomy morning, putting down his glasses and throwing aside one of the newspapers which for years had scorned him and now proclaimed him "America's greatest, most dazzling master of modern lyric drama." "Ezekiel, my esteemed friend, they have decided to *keep* the part of Olga Petrovna's rushing in as her husband is rising skyward to Paradise."

Ezekiel nodded. "I read it in the evening tabloid," he spoke loftily.

"Where on earth, do you suppose, *is* Olga," Abner wondered.

Ezekiel now produced a clipping from another tabloid and handed it to Abner.

"Oh, read it to me, Zeke, my eyes are smarting from all the newsprint I have been reading for days."

Ezekiel gave one of his put-upon gestures, but then began reading:

"The world-renowned silent screen star, Madame Olga Petrovna, has been confined to a sanitorium owing to a complete nervous collapse, according to her doctor."

"Stop," Abner groaned. "Oh, print, print, print!" he went on. "How in the world can anyone believe anything that is print."

Ezekiel waited for Abner to continue. Biting into a blueberry muffin, the composer went on:

"Madame Olga Petrovna was never so well-known as Madam Nazimova whom she aped shamelessly, and as to Olga's having a nervous collapse or whatever, Olga never knew a moment in her entire life that was not that of a born hysteric, melodramatist, and professional mad woman. Madness was always her forte, her *all* and her *only*. She, if given modern drugs to cure the madness that is her, would dissolve into a breeze as insubstantial as the indecent negligée she wore the other evening when, hoping to ruin my opera, she probably made its scandalous success sure."

"The photographers are here, Mr. Blossom," Malachi announced entering.

"Zeke, please write down in my ledger," Abner cried, "the record book is over there to your right, please write down what you say the hotel manager said today about success being as calamitous as failure, will you please?"

Long files of curiosity-seekers still lined the street in front of the Enrique at almost any hour, hoping to catch sight of the composer who had "shocked the socks off" the intellectual and popular worlds of apathetic anaesthetic little old New York.

As Abner looked out at the throngs, the words of the hotel manager kept coming to mind.

"Not so much calamitous perhaps," Abner would remark aloud, "as *inverosimile*, to use an Italian word. And finally quite a bore."

But as both success and scandal were slowly being digested by Abner and his friends and disciples, and when the crowds became a little thinner each day, a kind of dreamy somnolent calm came over the composer.

Faces of friends long dead were suddenly remembered, memories of days long past appeared, with Paris as the locale, or sometimes it was Tangier which flooded his brain.

Abner felt perhaps the way Val Sturgis had told him his Luigi had felt when enfolded in the love and splendor of his own idol, Francis X. Beauregard. And though Abner Blossom did not believe there was a hereafter, or a Good Shepherd waiting to usher him into paradise, he had the peculiar sensation he was somehow already in a kind of static heaven created out of his own world and work.

As in those old silent films he had watched enraptured as a boy and young man, the final title FINIS seemed to appear on the skyline as he looked down on the crowd of curiosity seekers outside, mostly black, mostly young, all beguiled perhaps into thinking he had written the long-awaited music drama just for them.

Abner felt there was no need to leave his apartment now or the Enrique. It was not invalidism or satiety or boredom, but again the sensation that comes to a voyager on a transatlantic ship which finally reaches port. The voyager for a few minutes wonders why he should trouble getting ashore when for six weeks or more he has had every want satisfied, every wish fulfilled, and his real home has been, he realizes, at sea and not on land.

Abner Blossom experienced a slow, steady and truly be-
atific feeling that all gifts had been bestowed on him, and nothing more need be vouchsafed to him.

"It can't be Easter already!" Abner complained to Malachi
and Ezekiel. "Look out at the weather. Snow then sleet, then
freezing rain, then all at once a stray beam of yellow sunlight!"

The snow, the freezing rain had thinned the crowds standing in front of the hotel. But it was not the freezing rain or thick
white snow that was afflicting Abner in so drastic a way. Every
night now he would wake up gasping, sometimes screaming.

"Nightmares at my age!" he would mumble.

Ezekiel now bade Malachi to sleep next to Abner on a cot
he had dragged out from one of the cavernous closets. But
during the first night he was to sleep in the same room with the
composer, Malachi complained the cot was too uncomfortable
and there were not enough blankets. Unbidden, Malachi
climbed into Abner's king-sized bed, but insisted on sleeping at
the foot of the bed.

"Why on earth do you want to sleep at the foot?"

"I ain't on your feet, am I?" Malachi chided, "so why
don't you let me stay where I am."

Abner mumbled something, and reached for the new restorative his own physician had given him. Tonight Abner tasted
the concoction with as much care as if he were correcting one of
his own scores. "Probably an opiate if not opium itself," he
muttered.

But whatever the new medicine was it did not keep away
the hobgoblins. Abner woke in the middle of the night choking
again and stifling screams.

"Did you think you saw something in the room?" Abner
sheepishly asked Malachi.

"Thought so, yes," Malachi admitted.

"You're sure?"

"I said I thought so."

"Who did you see?"

Malachi pulled the blanket up round his neck.

"Saw a white-haired gent with long front teeth and sharp sharp deep-brown eyes."

"You're not making this up, Malachi?"

"You asked me and I've told you."

Trying to go back to sleep again that night Abner Blossom this time either saw Cyril Vane come into the room or he dreamed he did, but on this the third visit of the "ghost" something got settled.

"You have forgotten," Cyril Vane began to speak now, "you have entirely failed to remember that years ago, Abner, in Paris when we could hear the German artillery and I had told you all about myself and my strange hidden world of forbidden loves – don't interrupt me now – I told you then in Paris you should one day write an opera about the real Cyril Vane."

"So you're not angry then I wrote *Cock Crow*," Abner cried sitting bolt upright in bed. "Here I thought all the time, Cyril, you had come to visit me because I had put you in an opera with all your forbidden secrets let loose at last."

"It's the Baptist in you, Abner," Cyril Vane seemed to speak again, dream or ghost or memory. "I wanted it more than anything else, to be in an opera. So go to sleep now and let that colored boy get some rest too."

And sleep Abner did after that. He realized too that for all his Paris years and his hobnobbing with the crowned heads of silent films, jazz greats, Grand Opera divas and a few gangsters, Cyril Vane had Abner's number, he was at least ninety percent Baptist, and his music came out of Baptist hymns, along with spirituals, blues and rag, and that was all of him and all there would ever be.

The Hotel Enrique must have let out a great sigh of relief when the crowds thinned out to one or two sightseers of an evening, the torch light processions stopped entirely, the young man who serenaded Abner with his harmonica disappeared, and the police no longer kept a trouble squad near the curb.

Abner Blossom had come into his own, and every night now, barring perhaps a Sunday when he slept day and night, there was nothing on his schedule but banquets, one right after the other. With money coming in "by the shovelfull," in his words, he even threatened to hire a fashionable French cook, but at the last moment changed his mind.

But he was already at work on a new opera which touched on a hero who was bound to be even more controversial and scandalous than Cyril Vane and his studio of black Adonises. For it was bruited about the new opera had for its story the Good Shepherd Himself and his Twelve Disciples and their own endless Banquets – brought of course up to date with a Baptist ring.